ABOUT THE AUTHOR

Geoff Wills is a former professional musician and clinical psychologist. His large-scale study of occupational stress in popular musicians, *Pressure Sensitive*, was published in 1988 and he has contributed to *International Musician* magazine, *jazz.com*, *Psychology of Music* and *The British Journal of Psychiatry*. In 2013 he contributed a chapter to the book *Frank Zappa and the And*.

ZAPPA AND JAZZ

DID IT REALLY SMELL FUNNY, FRANK?

GEOFF WILLS

Matador
9 Priory Business Park,
Wistow Road, Kibworth Beauchamp,
Leicestershire. LE8 0RX
Tel: 0116 279 2299
Email: books@troubador.co.uk
Web: www.troubador.co.uk/matador
Twitter: @matadorbooks

ISBN 978 1784623 913

British Library Cataloguing in Publication Data.
A catalogue record for this book is available from the British Library.

Printed and bound by CPI Group (UK) Ltd, Croydon, CR0 4YY
Typeset in Garamond by Troubador Publishing Ltd, Leicester, UK

Matador is an imprint of Troubador Publishing Ltd

For Judith

CONTENTS

AUTHOR'S NOTE

The world of popular music writing tends to be partisan. In general, rock writers don't write about jazz, and jazz writers don't write about rock. Of course, there are exceptions: Richard Williams writes eloquently about musicians as different as Miles Davis, Bruce Springsteen, Lou Reed and Duke Ellington, all in one volume, *Long Distance Call* (2000), and Barney Hoskyns includes excellent sections on West Coast jazz in his book about the Los Angeles rock and pop music scene *Waiting for the Sun* (1996). Bill Milkowski writes about personalities as diverse as Keith Richards, Wynton Marsalis and John Zorn in *Rockers, Jazzbos and Visionaries* (1999). But in general there tends to be little cross-fertilization of information, and this is unfortunate, especially when attempting to gain a complete picture of an artist like Frank Zappa. In this book I have attempted to present an example which helps to correct this imbalance.

CHAPTER 1

DID IT REALLY SMELL FUNNY?

With every year that has passed since his death in 1993 at the age of fifty two, there has been an increasing acceptance that Frank Zappa is an iconic musical figure. His music continues to be played by a variety of ensembles in America and Europe, and at the time of writing, twenty eight Zappa biographies or Zappa-related books are currently available. Although he used the arena of popular music to make his entrance into public consciousness, to class him simply as a popular musician would be to do him a severe disservice.

Zappa's music has a unique and easily recognizable quality, and is a brilliant and original synthesis of a wide range of cultural influences, including those of twentieth century classical music, film music, cartoon soundtracks, American stand-up comedy, rhythm and blues and jazz. This book focuses on just one of the influences on Zappa's music, namely jazz, and an attempt is made to clarify the often-confusing nature of his relationship with it. From the commencement of his career, and regularly thereafter, his liking for jazz (at least, certain types of jazz), and its influence on his work, was obvious. And yet Zappa liked to give the impression that he disliked jazz. On his album *Roxy and Elsewhere* (1973) he famously stated that 'jazz is not dead

1

… it just smells funny', and in his autobiography *The Real Frank Zappa Book* (1989) he included a section entitled 'Jazz: The Music of Unemployment.' In a 1978 interview with Dave Fass in *Acid Rock* magazine, he simply said 'I don't like jazz.' Possibly his most vehement statement on the topic occurred in a 1984 interview with Richard Cook in *New Musical Express*:

> I was never involved with jazz. There's no passion in it. It's a bunch of people trying to be cool, looking for certification of an intellectual community. Most of today's jazz is worth less than the most blatantly commercial music because it pretends to be something it's not. I'd rather stay away from that.
>
> *(Cook 1984, 15)*

In 2003 the music writer Charles Shaar Murray wrote and presented a programme for BBC Radio 3 about Zappa and jazz entitled *Jazz from Hell*. In it he took Zappa at his word and stated that 'Frank Zappa was not a jazz musician – and he obviously didn't see himself as one – he wasn't even a jazz fan.' In the present thesis, I shall attempt to show that this statement is manifestly untrue.

So why did Zappa say that he disliked jazz? In truth what he disliked was not jazz, but the *jazz Establishment*, just as he disliked every other Establishment, be it that of education, religion, politics, classical music or any other orthodoxy of American society. In this sense, he was a classic outsider. Quite simply, jazz was just one of a long list of subjects that had the capacity to incur his displeasure. One has only to refer to *The Real Frank Zappa Book* to encounter a continuous flow of irritants, including people ('stupidity, not hydrogen, is the basic building block of the universe … I don't have friends'), the education system ('I don't like teachers. I don't like schools'), politicians ('a bunch of really bad people'), musicians ('they tend to be lazy, and they get sick and skip rehearsals'), the tendency of symphony orchestra members to make mistakes ('… made so many mistakes, and played so badly … that it required forty edits … to try to cover them') and religion (**'The Cloud-Guy** who has **The Big Book'**).

How did Zappa acquire these bleak views? From an early age his experiences gave him good reason to be cautious in his dealings with the world. As Barry Miles (2004) observes, at the end of the Second World War, people did not forget that Italy had been at war with America, and the young Zappa, as an Italian-American, was subject to bullying. Between the ages of five and ten he was a sickly child, and as a youth his appearance was the antithesis of the all-American boy: he told Kurt Loder (1990) that when he was eleven, he weighed about 180 pounds, had big pimples and a moustache. To add to his feelings of insecurity, his father, ostensibly because of his work, had caused his family to move home eleven times by the time Zappa was aged eighteen.

In *The Real Frank Zappa Book* he says 'Because of my dad's work, I switched from school to school fairly often. I didn't enjoy it … I kept getting thrown out of high school … I had gotten to hate education so much, I was so fed up with going to school …' His relationship with his father became strained: 'I didn't get along all that well with him

… Mostly I tried to stay out of his way – and I think he tried to stay out of mine as much as he could …' Barry Miles (2004) discusses Zappa's father, and suggests that there was an agitated quality in his inability to settle in one job for too long, leading to constant, unnecessary relocation. This had a detrimental effect on his family, who found it increasingly difficult to make an emotional commitment to anything more than superficial friendships in each new setting. The young Frank became withdrawn, inward-looking and wary of letting his real feelings show, and this was a mindset that cast a shadow for the rest of his life. By the time he was fifteen he had attended six separate high schools, predictably affecting his education negatively and precluding entry to a university, even though he was highly intelligent.

In his Zappa biography *No Commercial Potential* (1996), David Walley quotes Ernest Tossi, vice-principal at Antelope Valley High School, as saying 'Frank was an independent thinker who couldn't accept the Establishment's set of rules.' In 1965 Zappa was falsely accused of making a pornographic tape and subsequently spent ten days in jail. Barry Miles comments that he was a changed man after this experience. Disillusioned by what he perceived to be the reactionary American system of education and government, he vowed that never again would he be taken in.

Because of his early life experiences, Zappa developed a personality with a distinctive set of traits. He had a distrust and suspiciousness of others, and was reluctant to confide in people because of a fear that the information would be used against him. He was unforgiving of slights, and because he was waiting for potential threats, he could act in a guarded or secretive manner. Hostile, sarcastic expressions were frequent, and it was not easy for him to accept criticism.

Thus, his scathing opinions often acted as smoke screens and defence mechanisms, so that while he was saying one thing he was doing another. For instance, although he could be scornful about film music, saying that it was '... so transparent. There's hardly any challenge in that' in 'The Mother of all Interviews' with Don Menn (1993), and parodying what he felt were its clichés and mannerisms in the extended version of his orchestral piece 'Bogus Pomp' (1987), he was also a good friend of the eminent film composer David Raksin, as the latter stated in an interview with Bruce Duffie (1988). And although Zappa stated that 'books make me sleepy,' he was well-read. Barry Miles describes how, as an adolescent, he read his father's books and then began frequenting the Lancaster County library in his search for alternative ideas and values. He was familiar with the works of Franz Kafka, William Burroughs, Philip K. Dick and Thomas Pynchon, according to Nigey Lennon (1995). It was as though he was worried that he might be caught out joining the Establishment, and then subjected to derision. And so it was with jazz. While criticizing it, he drew on its influences. It is no wonder that pianist George Duke, in Charles Shaar Murray's previously-mentioned radio programme, was moved to comment that 'it was always interesting to me, why he had this reticence about jazz, and at the same time, there was jazz going on all around him. I thought there was something strange about that, but he wouldn't admit it.' And in the same programme keyboard player Tommy Mars felt that, for Zappa, jazz was 'like that thing in the closet.'

The eminent American composer John Adams, discussing Zappa in a 2002 BBC Radio 3 interview, said:

> One of his goals in life was to prove that he could do anything – you know, you wanna play blues guitar? I'll beat ya at that! You wanna have a gross- out contest? I'll beat ya at that! You wanna write super-complex avant-garde European music? I can do that too!
>
> *(Adams 2002, BBC Radio 3)*

Zappa was trying to show that he was better than the Establishment that had slighted him. The phrase (with apologies to Shakespeare) 'He doth protest too much, methinks' springs to mind here, and it is sad because he had nothing to prove: his brilliance was apparent.

CHAPTER 2

EARLY ENCOUNTERS WITH JAZZ

When, at the age of fourteen, Zappa entered Mission Bay High School in San Diego in 1955, his first exposure to the elitist snobbery of a certain type of jazz fan occurred. It was like a red rag to a bull, and was no doubt the source of all his later caustic comments about jazz. He recounted the experience in an interview with Dan Forte in *Musician* magazine in 1979: '… at the time I was down there, there was a real definite division between the people who liked rhythm and blues and the people who liked jazz … The people who liked jazz would always go around putting you down …' These people were fans of West Coast jazz, at the time at the height of its popularity, and exemplified by Howard Rumsey's Lighthouse All-Stars and Shorty Rogers and his Giants. Unfortunately, Zappa's ire at mindless adherence to a fashion spilled over onto the music. He commented '… to me, there wasn't that much emotional depth in listening to something like 'Martians Go Home' by Shorty Rogers – that kind of stuff. It was just bleak.'

Was Zappa being disingenuous here? 'Martians Go Home' is not bleak – it is a piece of quirkily mischievous, Basie-inspired, small-group swing. Interestingly, Rogers, like many West Coast jazz musicians, also had a foot in the rhythm and blues camp. He supervised recording sessions by doo-wop groups and formed a publishing company with singer Jesse Belvin, publishing the latter's hit 'Guess Who' (Rounce, 2004). Under the name Boots Brown and the Blockbusters he recorded a series of rhythm and blues instrumentals and reached number 23 in the charts in 1958 with 'Cerveza' (Myers, 2013). It is not stretching the imagination too much to suggest that Rogers was the type of person that Zappa later sought to emulate when he worked with Paul Buff at Pal Studios in the early 1960s, where they produced rock instrumentals and used group names like The Hollywood Persuaders and The Rotations.

Jazz fans could be bigoted and snobbish. So could certain jazz musicians. On the other hand, many were prepared to be open-minded about different types of music. They were not all haters of rhythm and blues.

Johnny Otis, who, as Barry Miles states, Zappa first met in 1958 on a visit to his studio, was another musician whose feet were in the camps of both jazz and rhythm and blues. He had early associations with jazz, having played drums with Lester Young, Illinois Jacquet and (at least according to Tom Lord's 2004 Jazz Discography) Stan Kenton. His experiences are recounted in his 1993 autobiography. Fans created rigid categories, but for the pragmatic musician, the boundaries between jazz and other types of music were much more fluid. Session bass player Carol Kaye, in a 1998 article in *Downbeat* magazine, admitted that although 'rock and roll was a dirty word among L.A. bebop musicians in the late 1950s ... if it hadn't been for the huge hidden jazz influence in the 1960s hits, that musical era might never have happened ...'

As described in the 1979 *Musician* interview, Zappa's first encounter with bebop was not a positive one. He said, 'I didn't hear any bebop until I moved away from San Diego, and moved to Lancaster and I came across a Charlie Parker album. I didn't like it – because it sounded very tuneless, and it didn't feel like it had any balls to it.' He confirmed these early impressions in later interviews: in 'The Mother of All Interviews' (Menn, 1993) he said, 'I didn't like Charlie Parker. I didn't like some other modern jazz things. Listening to these things, I would go, "Why do people like this? I don't understand it".' And in the *Zappa Late Show Special* on BBC 2 TV in 1993, in his interview with Nigel Leigh he said:

> I'd come into contact with Charlie Parker records and things like that, but they didn't hold my interest. I couldn't follow it. Same kind of argument that you'd get from people today: 'What are they doing? They're just noodling around,' you know. I mean, now I understand why they're noodling and where they're noodling and I can tell the difference between good noodling and bad noodling, but without certain musical clues, it just all sounded like noodles to me.
>
> *(Leigh 1993, BBC2 TV)*

Zappa was only fifteen when he first encountered Parker's music. In 'The Mother of All Interviews', he described how and why he struggled to understand and appreciate certain pieces of music, for instance 'Chronochromie' by Olivier Messiaen:

It's just that the more I learned, the more interesting it became, because at the time I was exposed to this kind of music, I didn't have a classical education. I was just a guy buying records. Everything that I liked was based on my gut reaction to what was on the record. For some reason I liked Varèse right away. I liked Stravinsky right away, but these other things not ... when you start learning about structure, when you start learning about how these things work, then you can appreciate how other people deal with the material ... the more I learned about what the rules of the game were, the more I could appreciate how other people might solve the problem.

(Menn 1993, 58)

Although he did not clarify this, it seems not unlikely that the more Zappa learned about music, the more his appreciation of Parker, like that of Messiaen, grew. His initial dislike of Parker may have been partly connected to aversive experiences with bebop-loving jazz snobs, in contrast to his reaction to the music of Varèse, as he said in the BBC 2 *Late Show Special*:

I liked it a lot. Nobody had to explain it to me ... It just sounded good to me. The dissonance – the way I perceived the dissonance was, 'these chords are *really mean*. I like these chords. And the drums are playing *loud* in this music, and you can hear the drums *often* in this music' ...

(Leigh 1993, BBC2 TV)

Contrasting with jazz snobs, Varèse, with his 'really mean' chords, loud drums and (according to *The Real Frank Zappa Book*) mad scientist looks, could express Zappa's teenage angst brilliantly, and was probably a perfect alternative to his father.

Despite his initial negative reaction to bebop, Zappa continued to explore jazz and invested in albums by Oscar Pettiford and Charles Mingus, according to the 1979 *Musician* article. He thought Pettiford was good, and really liked Mingus. He also liked Thelonious Monk, Eric Dolphy and Harold Land. These were not musicians that the casual fan would be familiar with – Zappa was obviously taking a serious interest. And all the jazz musicians that he professed to like had moved through the bebop experience to develop their own music. Ted Gioia (1992) states that 'the music [Dolphy] was playing on gigs in the mid-1950s was ... closely related to the bebop idiom.' Pettiford, Mingus and Monk all played with Parker at different times. In Lancaster, Zappa became a student at Antelope Valley High School, and, as Barry Miles (2004) describes, he explored its record library. Here he became familiar with albums by Ornette Coleman and Cecil Taylor, and later developed a liking for the Oliver Nelson album *Blues and the Abstract Truth* (1961), featuring Eric Dolphy. He became a jazz autodidact, in the same way that he taught himself about twentieth century classical music.

Zappa referred to another jazz album that he was familiar with in a 1967 interview with Frank Kofsky. He was asked if he listened to John Coltrane and he replied:

Well, I don't own any Coltrane, except he's one artist on
the anthology album that Tom Wilson produced in 1950
[it was actually 1957]. The one that has Cecil Taylor and
Sun Ra. It's called *Jazz in Transition* – it's a classic.

(Kofsky 1967, 28-32)

This album features Sun Ra and Cecil Taylor at relatively
conventional stages in their careers, and John Coltrane in a
mid-1950s hard bop setting reminiscent of his *Blue Train*
session. Other tracks include one with Donald Byrd,
featuring Horace Silver and Art Blakey, and Boston groups
led by Dick Wetmore, Jay Migliori and Herb Pomeroy (the
album was recorded in Boston to showcase Wilson's
Transition label). So here was Zappa enthusing about an
album containing a mixture of 1950s modern and early
avant-garde jazz.

Zappa was on his own ceaseless personal, private quest
to gather knowledge and information that would feed into
his unique vision – the Project/Object, the overall concept
of his work in various mediums, with each project
connecting to a larger object. It appears that he made regular
'research trips', exemplified by his visit to Johnny Otis's
studio in 1958, and, having discovered Miles Davis ('I really
liked his music,' he said in a 1984 *RockBill* magazine interview
with Robert O'Brian), he went to see him play at the Black
Hawk in San Francisco. Sadly, when Zappa introduced
himself to Davis, the latter turned his back – typical Davis
behaviour that consolidated Zappa's experience with the San
Diego jazz fans and undoubtedly increased his misgivings
about certain aspects of jazz. 'I haven't had anything to do

with him or his music since that time' said Zappa. But at least he did admit that he had liked Davis's music (incidentally, although Zappa described the meeting as happening in 1962, there is no record of Davis appearing at the Black Hawk in that year, so it was probably the previous year, when Davis's historic *Friday Night/Saturday Night at the Blackhawk* albums were recorded).

It is interesting to speculate about other research trips that Zappa might have made. As Vladimir Simosko states in his 1974 biography of Eric Dolphy, the Ojai, California, Festival in 1962 featured Dolphy playing Varèse's 'Density 21.5', and other performers included Cathy Berberian and Luciano Berio. Compositions by John Cage and Thelonious Monk were played. This is the sort of event that Zappa might have attended but not talked about. Certainly, Zappa associates like trumpeter Malcolm McNab were involved in the Ojai Festival during the early 1960s. McNab discusses this in the notes for *Wazoo* (2007). Interestingly, Zappa had Cathy Berberian in mind as a singer when he wrote a piece of music in 1968 entitled 'Music for the Queen's Circus' which later became *200 Motels*. Zappa's widow Gail discussed this at a talk given prior to the 2013 London performance of *200 Motels* (Greenaway, 2014).

One also wonders whether Zappa paid a visit to The Lighthouse in Hermosa Beach, despite his disparaging comments about Howard Rumsey's Lighthouse All Stars (as well as referring to them in the 1979 Musician interview, he sarcastically called them 'Howard Ramsey's Light Love All Stars' in the 1967 Frank Kofsky interview, so he was familiar with their music). A number of black groups, playing funky, soulful hard bop that would have appealed to Zappa, recorded live albums there. They included those of Cannonball Adderley in 1960 and The Jazz Crusaders and Curtis Amy, both in 1962. After appearing at the Lighthouse, Amy hired the crisp, swinging drummer Ron Selico, who played on Zappa's classic track 'Peaches en Regalia' in 1969. Selico can be heard with Amy, recorded on the 1962 KTLA TV programme *Frankly Jazz*, on the 2008 Dupree Bolton CD *Fireball*. Fellow Californian musicians like John Densmore, who became the drummer with The Doors, were familiar with The Lighthouse. Densmore, as reported by Harvey Kubernik in 2009, said:

> I saw every jazz great who came to town the first half of the 1960s. Les McCann at the Renaissance Club. Cannonball Adderley at Howard Rumsey's Lighthouse. Bill Evans five or six times at Shelly's Manne Hole.
>
> *(Kubernik 2009, 84)*

Another fact worth noting is that, around the time that Zappa was becoming aware of the music of the composer who became his favourite, Edgard Varèse, the latter was forming close associations with New York jazz musicians. He was on friendly terms with Charlie Parker until the latter's death in 1955, as he described in Robert Reisner's book *Bird: The Legend of Charlie Parker* (1962), and was involved in a series of jam sessions in 1957, organized by composer Earle Brown. Eminent jazz musicians participating included Art Farmer (trumpet), Frank Rehak (trombone), Hal McKusick (clarinet and alto saxophone),

Teo Macero (tenor saxophone), Hall Overton (piano), Charles Mingus (bass) and Ed Shaughnessy (drums). Olivia Mattis (2006) gives a comprehensive account of these sessions, and bassist Bill Crow discusses the meetings in his 1993 book *From Birdland to Broadway*. The improvised nature of the music occurred four years before Ornette Coleman's album *Free Jazz* (1961) was released. Might Zappa have been aware of Varèse's jazz associations?

CHAPTER 3

FIRST JAZZ RECORDINGS

It seems significant that when Frank Zappa made his first excursion into a legitimate recording studio, it was to make a bona-fide jazz record. The year was 1961, and the studio was Pal Records in Cucamonga, California. The studio owner, Paul Buff, as reported by Rip Rense in 1996, said:

> He just came in one day in 1960, when he was around 20, as a person who wanted to record some jazz. He had some musicians, and wanted to rent a studio. Probably the first year or so I was associated with him he was doing a combination of recording jazz, producing some jazz records, and was also writing some symphonic material for a large orchestra that was supposed to record some of it. He was very jazz-oriented … He played clubs, and played all the jazz standards…
>
> *(Rense 1996, 15)*

In January 1961 Zappa recorded an original composition entitled 'Never On Sunday', which later became known as 'Take Your Clothes off When You Dance'. The track eventually appeared on the 1996 album *The Lost Episodes*. He was accompanied on the session by Chuck Foster (trumpet),

Tony Rodriquenz (alto saxophone), Danny Helferin (piano), Caronga Ward (bass), and Chuck Glave (drums). 'Never On Sunday/Take Your Clothes off When You Dance' is an excellent piece of straight-ahead jazz, with strong solos all round. Chuck Foster makes a clean, arresting statement with a broadly Dizzy Gillespie/Clifford Brown sound, while altoist Tony Rodriquenz is excitingly reminiscent of Cannonball Adderley and Phil Woods (and is also obviously influenced by Charlie Parker, whose music Zappa said 'didn't feel like it had any balls to it'). Danny Helferin's piano style is somewhat like that of Jack Wilson, who was making a name on the West Coast around the time this was recorded. Frank Zappa's rhythm playing is perfect for the music. Interestingly, the tune is a bossa nova, and was recorded a year before Stan Getz made this form popular with 'Desafinado'. The music fits perfectly with other jazz that was happening on the West Coast in the early 1960s: funky, soulful music played by musicians like Les McCann, Harold Land, Curtis Amy and the Jazz Crusaders.

The author interviewed trumpeter Chuck Foster in 2008, and he remembered rehearsing with Zappa at Pal Studios for a couple of weeks, saying 'It was real loose, we had a lot of laughs, a very relaxed atmosphere. Oh yes, Frank always liked jazz – he was always a fan.' Foster said of altoist Tony Rodriquenz, 'He was a monster – sounded like Cannonball Adderley. But he gravitated away from music and became a teacher (not music) and played at weekends.' Sadly, Rodriquenz died of cancer in 2007. Foster worked with Zappa again in 1963 when he recorded the latter's score for the movie *Run Home Slow*, and later worked with Si Zentner,

Della Reese, Buddy Rich and Harry James. He recorded his own album, *Long Overdue*, in 1985.

The author also interviewed drummer Chuck Glave in 2008, and he remembered playing a number of dates with Zappa in the early 1960s. He specifically recalled playing at Zappa's father's restaurant, when Zappa was trying to play jazz on vibraphone. This was around 1963. Glave, who since the 1980s has been a member of the Regency Jazz Band, a San Antonio hard bop outfit, remembered that Zappa was definitely a jazz fan at this time.

According to Greg Russo (2012) another track was recorded at the same session as 'Never On Sunday', featuring Chuck Foster, trumpet, Tony Rodriquenz, also on trumpet rather than alto sax, Frank Zappa on guitar and Chuck Glave on drums. When the author spoke to Foster, he had no memory of this recording, or of Rodriquenz playing trumpet, but one assumes that Russo is acting on information from Paul Buff. The track was called 'High Steppin'' and later appeared, speeded up and retitled 'It's From Kansas', on the album *Lumpy Gravy*. Preserved only on a crackly-sounding acetate, 'High Steppin'' has a 32-bar theme, with a repeated 16-bar phrase, which sounds like a cross between the 1930 song 'Bye Bye Blues' and the 1918 song 'After You've Gone'. It is not unlike something Bix Beiderbecke might have done. Zappa knew the jazz standards, even if he made fun of them. Certainly, the comments by Buff, Foster and Glave directly contradict Charles Shaar Murray's 2003 statement that Zappa was not a jazz fan.

CHAPTER 4

JOE PERRINO AND THE II-V-I EXPERIENCE

For about nine months from November 1961, Zappa played with a lounge group called Joe Perrino and the Mellotones. Much of the repertoire consisted of popular standards, and because he had to play them with mediocre musicians in seedy environments to unappreciative audiences, he developed extremely negative feelings about them. He discussed with Frank Kofsky how:

> I was ... working in what you might call a tiptoe-through-the-tulips-type band, wearing a white tuxedo coat ... black pants, black patent-leather shoes, hair slicked back, choreography, played three twist numbers a night, and the rest of the stuff was "Oh How We Danced on the Night"...
>
> *(Kofsky 1967, 28-32)*

In the 1993 BBC 2 *Late Show Special* he said 'you had to read songs out of a thick brown book, flip the pages in the dark and see what the chord changes were. Nobody else in the band really knew the chord changes.' The experience engendered in Zappa a hatred of the II-V-I chord progression, which is used in a wide variety of

musical styles, especially jazz. Speaking with Frank
Kofsky, he called it 'the same subconscious formula that
all those pukers [popular songwriters] use', and in the
1979 *Musician* magazine interview he referred to 'that
moron II-V-I syndrome ... those goddamn jazz guys with
II-V-I ... the bottom line of white person music.' So, at a
stroke, he seemingly dismissed the entire American
popular songbook. The song 'America Drinks and Goes
Home', which appears on the album *Absolutely Free*, uses
the II-V-I progression, and is a parody of his lounge-
music experience, with inane lyrics and the sound of
drunken audience members. Zappa described it as 'a very
scientific parody of that genre ... It's not a bad tune.' In
actual fact it is an *excellent* tune, and stands up very well
without needing to be a parody. With regard to this, it is
interesting to listen to straight-ahead jazz versions by the
Woody Herman Orchestra (1974), Riccardo Fassi and the
Tankio Band (1994) and Mark Kross with Herb Pomeroy
(1990).

Why did Zappa need to carry out a 'very scientific' study
of something he supposedly hated? He was humiliated by
his lounge-music ordeal – uncaring audiences, anodyne
surroundings, perhaps being criticized by an insensitive
musician for supposedly playing the wrong chords – and he
added it to his other aversive life experiences. Again he
'protested too much', venting his spleen on the popular
music and jazz Establishments, and as the previously-quoted
John Adams might have said: 'You wanna write a II-V-I
song? I'll beat ya at that, too!' Brett Clement, in his 2009
study of Zappa's instrumental music, comments:

> One peculiar fallout of this [lounge] experience was
> Zappa's distaste for jazz music. Though we know jazz to
> be one of the key stylistic categories for his instrumental
> music, Zappa chose to equate the term 'jazz' with a
> relatively limited corpus, namely the jazz standards and
> bebop repertoire.
>
> *(Clement 2009. 102)*

Zappa continued to take pot-shots at standards throughout his career, for instance quoting from 'Midnight Sun' in 'Nanook Rubs It' (1974) and 'Isn't It Romantic' in 'Punky's Whips' (1978). The melody of 'Flambay' (1979) combines elements of 'Laura' and 'Fly Me to the Moon'. But whether he liked it or not, Zappa had the capacity to write legitimate jazz tunes. In a personal communication with the author in 2008, Paul Buff stated:

> The main deal with Frank was that he never aspired to be
> a part of any movement or group – he was his own man.
> Thus, if the jazz community shunned him it was natural
> he would give them the finger and do his own thing …
> it's clear he didn't abandon jazz – he refined it with his
> own signature.
>
> *(Buff 2008)*

Buff also felt, as quoted by Rip Rense in 1996, that Zappa switched from making jazz-oriented to more novel records in order to get on the Steve Allen TV Show as a means of furthering his career. This he did in March 1963 with his bicycle-playing stunt.

CHAPTER 5

ZAPPA AND THE JAZZ WALTZ

An increasingly popular phenomenon in jazz from the 1950s onwards was the jazz waltz. Some examples of this include 'Valse Hot' by Sonny Rollins (1956), 'Some Day My Prince Will Come' by Dave Brubeck (1957), 'My Favorite Things' by John Coltrane (1961), 'This Here' by Bobby Timmons (1960) and 'West Coast Blues' by Wes Montgomery (1960). Frank Zappa appeared to be especially enamoured of this form, and there are numerous examples in his work. An early excursion into 3/4 occurred in one of the themes in his 1961 music for the movie *The World's Greatest Sinner*, and this theme was later used in 'Holiday in Berlin', on the album *Burnt Weeny Sandwich* (1970). However, his first serious attempt at a jazz waltz occurred in January 1963 at Pal Studio, when he recorded his own composition, simply titled 'Waltz' (Buff, 2012). On this he played everything – lead guitar, rhythm guitar, bass and drums – and the piece has a modal jazz waltz feeling similar to that of, for instance, 'My Favorite Things' or 'Greensleeves' by John Coltrane. Zappa plays a modal vamp on rhythm guitar similar to McCoy Tyner's piano work on the above-mentioned Coltrane titles, and his drumming shows the influence of Elvin Jones. Although the recording is only a demo, and Zappa's guitar solo is somewhat hesitant at times, the modal jazz influences on his music at this time are strongly apparent.

Zappa's next jazz waltz was first recorded in 1964 as part of his teenage opera *I Was a Teen-age Malt Shop*, and came to be known as 'Toads of the Short Forest'. It appears on the album *Beat the Boots III*, Disc One (2009). Again, he probably played everything – guitar, piano, bass and drums – on this recording. A wistfully endearing tune, it was recorded again in 1969 and appeared on the album *Weasels Ripped My Flesh*. Jazz musician Ed Palermo, whose big band has recorded a number of Zappa tribute albums, said of it in 2007:

> His melodies just seem to come out of nowhere, but make perfect musical sense. A song like 'Toads of the Short Forest' … is a great example. A jazz waltz, the melody of which is played by an acoustic guitar through a wah- wah pedal (who else would have thought of that?) flies effortlessly through a complex array of chord changes.
>
> *(Palermo 2007, 1)*

And in a 2009 interview with Michael Bourne, Palermo commented on how intrigued by the chord changes eminent tenor saxophonist Bob Mintzer was when playing a solo on the tune. Nigey Lennon (2003) felt that 'the tune is one of the most effective guitar pieces I've heard by anybody.'

Some other examples of Zappa's use of the jazz waltz format include 'The Idiot Bastard Son', 'King Kong' (actually in 3/8), 'The Eric Dolphy Memorial Barbecue', 'Twenty Small Cigars', 'Blessed Relief', 'For Calvin' and 'RDNZL'.

Regarding 'King Kong', Ed Palermo (2007) commented that

> You can tell … by listening to so much of his music that
> he really loved jazz. … listening to a modal masterpiece
> like 'King Kong' proves, at least to my ears, that he had
> listened to and digested a lot of Miles and Trane.
>
> *(Palermo 2007)*

Ted Gioia (2009) felt that 'Blessed Relief'

> … is a catchy jazz waltz that could almost pass for a Blue
> Note hard bop chart. Sal Marquez and George Duke
> contribute first-rate solos, and Zappa follows with some
> tasty guitar lines that are very, very jazzy.
>
> *(Gioia 2009)*

This latter observation contradicts Zappa's 1967 statement
– one of his smoke-screens – that 'I can't play jazz worth a
shit and I would never claim to.' Incidentally, 'Blessed Relief',
though in no way a copy, perfectly conjures the mood of the
Frank Rosolino-composed jazz standard 'Blue Daniel',
recorded by, among others, Shelly Manne (1959) and
Cannonball Adderley (1960).

CHAPTER 6

EARLY ENCOUNTERS WITH STUDIO MUSICIANS

1963 was a significant year for Zappa because at this time he experienced his first major encounters with musicians who worked mainly in studio or orchestral settings, and who frequently had a background in jazz. These encounters continued regularly throughout Zappa's career, and included the sessions for the albums *Freak Out* (1966), *Absolutely Free* (1967), *Lumpy Gravy* (1968), *Hot Rats* (1969), *200 Motels* (1971), *Waka/Jawaka* (1972), *The Grand Wazoo* (1972), *Studio Tan* (1978) and *Orchestral Favorites* (1979). The musicians were always impressed by Zappa's ability and musicianship, as is demonstrated, for instance, by the comments of percussionist Emil Richards in the sleeve notes for *Lumpy Money* (2008), in relation to the original orchestral sessions for *Lumpy Gravy* in 1967. But, for his part, Zappa was often disparaging about musicians who had a thorough academic background. For instance, in a 1976 interview with Cherry Ripe in *New Musical Express*, he referred to the members of his first 1973 band as 'boring' and wrote a song about them called 'Po-jama People'. This seems to be further evidence of his ambivalent, conflicted feelings, and his need to retaliate against the musical Establishment.

Zappa's first 1963 encounter with session musicians occurred when he appeared on the Steve Allen Show in March of that year to perform his piece 'Concerto for Two Bicycles'. As part of the performance he asked the resident Donn Trenner Orchestra to play in a random manner, creating, in effect, a piece of free jazz. Incidentally, Zappa's performance was very reminiscent of the one that composer John Cage gave on the CBS prime time TV game show *I've got a Secret* in January 1960, when he performed his piece 'Water Walk' using a water pitcher, an iron pipe, a goose call, a bottle of wine and an electric mixer.

On May 19, 1963 Zappa gave a concert of his experimental music at Mount St. Mary's College, Claremont, California, which was later broadcast on radio station KPFK. Gordon Skene (2010) gives details on his *Weekend Gallimaufry* website. The music was played by an ensemble billed as the Pomona Valley Symphony Orchestra, and among its members was trumpeter Malcolm McNab, who later became an eminent studio musician. This was the first of many times that the latter worked with Zappa, who in 1972 composed a piece for him entitled, appropriately, 'The Malcolm McNab'. This later became 'Be-Bop Tango'. One of the items performed at the concert, named 'Piece Number Two of Visual Music 1957 for Jazz Ensemble and 16 mm Projector', was an avant-garde jazz piece featuring a woodwind section including flute, alto and baritone saxophones, and a rhythm section of piano, bass and drums. The listener is struck by how accomplished the playing is, with vigorous 'free' drumming, and how reminiscent the piece is of 'Abstraction', an example of Third Stream music by Gunther Schuller recorded in 1960 and featuring Ornette Coleman. Another work performed at the concert, entitled 'Piano Pieces from Opus 5', hints in places at the work of Thelonious Monk and Cecil Taylor.

In 1959 Zappa had been commissioned to write the score for a low-budget western called *Run Home Slow*, but due to financial problems experienced by the film's producer, the film was not completed and scored until 1963, as *The Real Frank Zappa Book* recounts. Excerpts from the score appear on *The Lost Episodes* (1996). The recording of the score took place at Original Sound Studios in Hollywood, and the musicians, all with strong jazz and/or studio credentials, included Chuck Foster (trumpet), Ron Myers (trombone), Chick Carter (flute, tenor and baritone saxophone), Don Christlieb (bassoon), Pete Christlieb (tenor saxophone), Chuck Domanico (bass) and John Guerin (drums) (this was the personnel as remembered by Chuck Foster in a conversation with the author in 2008). This was Zappa's first meeting in the recording studio with John Guerin and Don Christlieb: the former would make an important contribution to Zappa projects such as *Hot Rats* (1969), and the latter, principal bassoon with Fox and MGM movie studios for many years, would appear on *Lumpy Gravy* (1968), Jean-Luc Ponty's *King Kong* (1970), *Studio Tan* (1978) and *Orchestral Favorites* (1979).

The score for *Run Home Slow* demonstrates that Zappa had listened closely to a great deal of movie music, and absorbed its principles. Some of the music is not unlike that for horror movies like Mario Bava's *The Mask of Satan* (1960), with a score for the American version by Les Baxter, and there is also a slow, haunting theme featuring Don Christlieb that turned up later as 'The Duke of Prunes' on *Absolutely Free* (1967). Perhaps of greatest interest is the Main Title theme, which Ben Watson (1994) refers to rather uncharitably as 'a passable cowboy-film overture: galloping drums and trumpets bursting with sunrise optimism.' The theme is in 3/4 and based on a minor pentatonic scale, with an ostinato featuring snare drum and marimba. The piece is in three sections, with the second section alternating between 3/4 and 4/4. The deguello-style trumpet solo and military snare pattern nod in the direction of Dimitri Tiomkin's Main Title theme from *The Alamo* (1960), and 'Saeta', from *Sketches of Spain* by Miles Davis (1960). This track is a key demonstration that as early as 1963, Zappa was producing interesting and complex music that challenged experienced session musicians, used varied time signatures and drew on a variety of influences, including jazz. And between 1961 and 1964, two years before the release of the first Mothers of Invention album in 1966, he had recorded jazz that drew on a variety of styles, including hard bop, the modal jazz waltz and the avant-garde.

CHAPTER 7

FREAK OUT

From a jazz point of view, the album *Freak Out* (1966) is interesting in a number of ways. In the sleeve notes, there is a list of names headed by the statement 'These people have contributed materially in many ways to make our music what it is. Do not hold it against them.' Included in the list are the names of jazz musicians Roland Kirk, Charles Mingus, Eric Dolphy, Cecil Taylor and Bill Evans. Zappa's appreciation of these musicians obviously contradicts his later statement to Richard Cook (1984) that 'I was never involved with jazz.'

At the end of the track 'The Return of the Son of Monster Magnet', there is a piano solo that is very reminiscent of Cecil Taylor, probably played by Zappa (in the 1967 Kofsky interview, he says he plays the piano solo on 'Help I'm a Rock', but as there is only a piano vamp on this track he is probably referring to 'Monster Magnet'). Pianist Les McCann, noted for his funky soul-jazz, was in the studio when *Freak Out* was recorded. He played on a track entitled 'Freak Trim', which only appeared later on the album *The Making of Freak Out* (2006).

A large group of session musicians was assembled for the recording of *Freak Out*. Vibraphonist Gene Estes (ex-Billy May, Shorty Rogers, Pete Rugolo, Louis Bellson) lent a jazzy sound to many tracks, and one wonders if Zappa savoured the irony of working with pianist Gene DiNovi, who had played with Dizzy Gillespie, Charlie Parker, Benny Goodman and Buddy Rich, and who had written songs recorded by people like Doris Day. Did he perhaps enjoy telling 'those goddamn jazz guys with II-V-I' what to do, after his experience with Joe Perrino and the Mellotones? The session musicians, for their part, were very appreciative of his work. Carol Kaye, a member of the famous Wrecking Crew group of session musicians, is quoted in the notes to *The Making of Freak Out* as saying '… the stuff was good. Frank knew what he wanted, and we loved that. You had respect for him, because you knew this kid had something.'

An eighteen-piece orchestra accompanied The Mothers on four *Freak Out* tracks. Zappa wrote the arrangements and conducted, and the results were impressive: he showed that, if he had been so inclined, he could have been a notable pop/rock session arranger similar to men like Jack Nitzsche or Ernie Freeman. Of course, that would have been too simple. Some of his orchestrations are reminiscent of the more melodic orchestral sections on the later *Lumpy Gravy* (1968). Also included in the orchestra were reed men Plas Johnson, Carol Kaye's frequent musical partner and previous member of Boots Brown's (Shorty Rogers's) Blockbusters, and another jazz orchestra musician, John Rotella (ex-Benny Goodman, Tommy Dorsey, Stan Kenton). The latter would record with Zappa again on a number of occasions.

Immediately prior to the recording of the next Mothers of Invention album, *Absolutely Free*, at the end of 1966, Zappa recruited two new band members, as Billy James

(2001) describes. Both had jazz backgrounds and both were around ten years older than the average rock group member of the era. Don Preston (born 21st September 1932) was an excellent jazz pianist and bass player who had worked with Herbie Mann, Elvin Jones, Tommy Flanagan, Yusef Lateef, Kenny Burrell, Pepper Adams, Nat King Cole, Shorty Rogers, Charlie Haden and Paul Bley. With such an impressive track record, it seems surprising that he did not stay purely in the jazz world – he was an exact contemporary of other West Coast jazz pianists of the time like Paul Bley and Pete Jolly – but he had eclectic tastes, being interested in electronic and avant-garde classical music, and he had constructed his own synthesiser in 1965. On *Absolutely Free* he can be heard on the track 'America Drinks and Goes Home', giving an accurate impersonation of a lounge pianist, with Erroll Garner-like flourishes and a solid jazz technique underlying the humour.

Preston had first met Frank Zappa in 1962, in the company of the other new recruit, multi-reed player Bunk Gardner. The latter was the younger brother of trumpeter Buzz Gardner, who Preston had roomed with while serving in the army in the early 1950s in Italy. Bunk Gardner (born 2nd May 1933) grew up in Cleveland, Ohio. After piano lessons from the age of five, he started to learn clarinet at age twelve, followed by tenor sax and oboe. He listened to modern jazz and classical music, and organized, with his brother, a dance band that played Stan Kenton arrangements. He later played with the Cleveland Philharmonic Orchestra. While in an army band at the time of the Korean War he was able to take part in jam sessions featuring Cannonball

Adderley and Junior Mance, and on his return to Cleveland he gained a BA in music. In 1959 Gardner recorded an album for the Roulette label with the Cleveland-based Bud Wattles Orchestra, entitled *Themes from the Hip* and featuring jazz versions of TV Western themes. On the album he can be heard playing competent tenor sax solos in the fashionable 'cool' style of the era. Also in the band was saxophonist Bobby Jones, who later worked with Charles Mingus. When Gardner moved to the West Coast with his brother Buzz he became acquainted with luminaries like comedian Lenny Bruce and alto saxophonist Joe Maini, but discographies do not mention him as recording with any name LA jazz groups. On the album *Absolutely Free* he can be heard on the track 'Invocation and Ritual Dance of the Young Pumpkin', playing a John Coltrane-influenced soprano sax solo against a modal vamp. In his 1967 Kofsky interview, Zappa commented 'We had to force him to play in that (Coltranesque) vein, when we had him in the band he was playing straight out of 1955.'

Another track on *Absolutely Free*, 'Brown Shoes Don't Make It', is interesting in that it features trumpeter and bandleader Don Ellis and multi-reed player John Rotella, the latter having worked with Zappa on *Freak Out*. Ellis, who was introduced to Zappa by his friend Don Preston, was making a name for himself on the West Coast leading a jazz orchestra which was noted for utilising odd time signatures and aspects of Indian music. Many Ellis ex-sidemen, including George Duke, Ralph Humphrey, Dave Parlato and Glenn Ferris later worked with Zappa.

CHAPTER 8

LUMPY GRAVY

As recounted in a 1979 interview with David Fricke in *Trouser Press* magazine, at the end of 1966 Zappa received an offer to record an album of his orchestral music from Capitol Records A & R man and producer Nick Venet. Recording sessions took place at Capitol Studios, Hollywood, in February and March 1967 with a large orchestra of studio musicians and Zappa participating in a purely composing and conducting role. Due to contractual difficulties between Capitol and Verve/MGM Records, the album, which came to be known as *Lumpy Gravy*, was not released on Capitol, but was finally released in altered form with additional non-orchestral material by Verve/MGM in 1968.

In 2009 the Zappa Family Trust released a three-disc set entitled *The Lumpy Money Project/Object* which contained Zappa's original orchestral edit of *Lumpy Gravy* for Capitol, the 1984 remix, and a series of out-takes containing previously unreleased material. Viewing this material as a whole, it transpires that, from a jazz point of view, *Lumpy Gravy* is one of Zappa's most interesting projects. The orchestra, from session sheets (Russo, 2003) and album sleeve notes, contained a number of eminent West Coast-based jazz/session musicians, including Jimmy Zito (trumpet), Kenny Shroyer or Lew McCreary (trombone), Ted Nash, Gene Cipriano and John Rotella (reeds), Paul Smith, Pete Jolly or Mike Lang (piano), Tommy Tedesco (guitar), Emil Richards or Victor Feldman (percussion), Jimmy Bond (bass), and Shelly Manne, Frank Capp or John Guerin (drums). According to the *Lumpy Money* liner notes the musicians initially felt that Zappa did not know what he was doing, but he quickly gained their respect. Guitarist Tommy Tedesco started off making fun of Zappa and ended by putting his arm round him and becoming a close friend. Again, Zappa was telling 'those goddamn jazz guys' what to do.

The *Lumpy Money* out-take 'How Did That Get In Here?', which contains some material that appeared on the Capitol and MGM versions of *Lumpy Gravy*, but much that did not, is of special interest. Incidentally, it is worth speculating on the recording date and the personnel for this track. Liner notes state that it was recorded on Sunday, 13th February 1967, but this date was actually a Monday. Session sheets state that the personnel was Paul Smith (piano), James Helms (guitar), Jimmy Bond (bass), Bob West (bass guitar), John Guerin (drums), Kenneth Watson (tympani, mallets), and Thomas Poole (percussion). However, trumpet, trombone, french horn, clavinet and rhythm guitar can also be heard. Paul Smith, a straight-ahead modern pianist who played in the style of Oscar Peterson and George Shearing, walked out of the session and was replaced by Mike Lang, according to Greg Russo (2003). The latter quotes Lang as saying 'I thought the music was wonderful – fresh, innovative, and completely unlike anything I had heard before.' The bassist and drummer definitely sound like Bond and Guerin, but a guitar solo sounds remarkably like the work of Tommy Tedesco and vibraphone work like that of Emil Richards. Sleeve notes state that the track 'is an FZ construction' so the given session date may not be the only one. All this sounds very nit-picking, but it is an attempt to gain some clarity in the frequently-confusing area of Zappa recording data.

'How Did That Get In Here?' is 25 minutes in length and is made up of a series of sections that vary in mood and tempo, segueing one into the next. The first section, lasting just over three minutes, uses thematic material from two of Zappa's movie scores, namely *The World's Greatest Sinner* and *Run Home Slow*, and the theme of what would later become the song 'Oh No', featured on the album *Weasels Ripped My Flesh* (1970). The instrumentation is piano, vibraphone, guitar, bass and drums, exactly that of the George Shearing Quintet, one of the most successful groups in jazz through the 1950s and 1960s, and sounding like Shearing playing jazz-fusion. Coincidentally, both Emil Richards and John Guerin had played with Shearing. The mood is initially cool, limpid and reflective, but moves into a statement of the 'Oh No' theme followed by a freak-out featuring trumpet, trombone and French horn. At 4:24 the music changes abruptly into a shuffle that seems to prefigure the introduction to the title tune of 1972's *The Grand Wazoo*, one of a number of indications on these out-takes that Zappa was already thinking in terms of big band jazz-rock. A further indication occurs at 5:58 when the music becomes 'Help I'm A Rock', from *Freak Out* (1966), with a jazz-rock sound not a million miles away from Blood, Sweat and Tears, although the latter band would not debut until later in 1967. Jimmy Zito, a dynamic lead and jazz trumpeter and a veteran of the bands of Tommy Dorsey, Les Brown and Benny Goodman, takes a strong, thoughtful solo. The combination of solo trumpet and 3/4 time signature harks back to the main title theme from *Run Home Slow*.

The long section that begins at 13:04 deserves special attention: it suggests that Zappa might have been listening to Sun Ra's 1965 album *Heliocentric Worlds*, especially the track 'Other Worlds'. A fast swing tempo features frantic drums, free-form horns, fuzz bass and dissonant piano. A cut to half-tempo showcases piano, vibraphone and trumpet, and is followed by an agitated avant-bop guitar solo, probably (as previously mentioned) by Tommy Tedesco. A military snare drum figure and trumpet give way once more to Cecil Taylor-type piano, mutating into a mixture of Varèse and avant-garde jazz that appeared on the original *Lumpy Gravy*. A slow, mysterious theme then eventually changes into the familiar 'Oh No' and the piece ends.

Another *Lumpy Money* out-take, titled 'Section 8, Take 22', presents the original version of one of Zappa's most popular themes, 'King Kong'. The instrumentation is trumpet, trombone, French horns and rhythm section featuring vibraphone, and the band initially plays with a loose big band jazz-rock-cum-Charles Mingus feel, with the 'King Kong' theme being played in 3/8 over a 4/4 rhythm. At 1:59 there is an abrupt switch into a fast 3/8 with the theme stated by trumpet and vibraphone, and shades of Mingus's 'Better Git It in Your Soul'.

Both the original Capitol version of *Lumpy Gravy* and the Verve/MGM version contain two orchestral suites which are chopped up and mixed together. One consists of excellent movie-type music that could be referred to as the 'Oh No Suite', while the other is 20th century orchestral music influenced by Varèse, Webern and Stravinsky. Hints of cool and avant-garde jazz also make appearances. It is only after hearing the *Lumpy Money* out-takes that the full extent of the jazz influences in the recordings is revealed: nods to George Shearing, big band jazz-rock, Charles Mingus and Sun Ra are all apparent. However ironic Zappa's intentions may have been regarding these influences, he was unable to stop himself from producing seriously good music.

CHAPTER 9

RESPECT FOR JAZZ MUSICIANS

In the year that *Lumpy Gravy* was recorded, Zappa paid his respects to a number of jazz musicians. In the August 1967 edition of *Hit Parader* magazine an article appeared which he had written entitled 'My Favorite Records'. He commenced the article by stating that

> If you want to learn how to play guitar, listen to Wes Montgomery. You should also go out and see if you can get a record by Cecil Taylor if you want to learn how to play the piano.
>
> *(Zappa 1967, 61)*

On the cover of the September 1967 edition of *Jazz & Pop* magazine, a photo appears of Zappa with tenor saxophonist Archie Shepp, and inside appears Zappa's previously-cited interview with Frank Kofsky. The article's introduction states that 'The Mothers include in their repertoire a composition by Zappa called "Archie's Home"', and features a photo of Shepp, who had come to hear a Mothers' gig, with Zappa and the Mothers, seemingly forming a mutual admiration society. In 1984 Shepp sat in with Zappa, and can be heard on volume 4 of *You Can't Do That On Stage Anymore*.

From March to September of 1967 Zappa and the Mothers had a residency at the Garrick Theatre on Bleecker Street in New York. For part of the time the Joe Beck Quartet, featuring vibraphonist Mike Mainieri, was playing beneath the Garrick in the Café Au Go Go. Mainieri, who had worked with Buddy Rich, Benny Goodman, Coleman Hawkins and Wes Montgomery, was an admirer of Zappa. He said:

> On Saturday afternoons we had creative music parties at the Garrick Theatre. We'd bring pieces we'd composed – Zappa, me, Don Preston and Joe Beck were involved, too. We might get a string quartet, other chamber instrumentalists, free blowers, whatever.

> *(Mainieri 1995, 5)*

Mainieri's experimentation and jamming with a variety of musicians evolved, by the late 1960s, into the White Elephant big band, a breeding ground for many musicians involved with jazz-rock, including the Brecker brothers, Ronnie Cuber, Steve Gadd and Tony Levin. In 1995 Mainieri recorded a version of Zappa's 'King Kong' on his album *An American Diary*, which was a tribute to American composers including, as well as Zappa, Leonard Bernstein, Aaron Copland, Roger Sessions and Samuel Barber.

Guitarist Joe Beck, who Mainieri played with at the Au Go Go, later appeared on the Gil Evans album *Blues in Orbit*, referred to in Chapter 16 in relation to *The Grand Wazoo*. It is interesting to speculate how much of his Zappa experience Beck was able to transmit to Evans.

CHAPTER 10

IAN UNDERWOOD, ART TRIPP AND UNCLE MEAT

As recounted in a 1977 *Downbeat* interview with Lee Underwood, in July 1967 another musician with a jazz background was recruited into the Mothers by Zappa. Ian Underwood (born 22nd May 1939) was nineteen months older than Zappa and came from a wealthy upper-middle-class background. Son of an executive for Republic Steel, he grew up on the North Shore of Long Island Sound, New York, and started classical piano lessons aged five. At the age of fourteen he was listening to Charlie Parker, Miles Davis, Horace Silver and Jackie McLean, and was starting to learn flute, clarinet, alto and tenor saxophones. After high school he attended the exclusive Choate Prep School in Connecticut and became friendly with fellow student and bass player Steve Swallow, practising regularly with him. In 1959, Underwood won a Schaefer Scholarship to the Lenox, Massachusetts, Summer Jazz School, and recorded with the Jimmy Giuffre ensemble, the Herb Pomeroy ensemble featuring Ornette Coleman and Gary McFarland, and the Kenny Dorham ensemble featuring Ornette Coleman, Don Cherry and John Bergamo (who later recorded with Zappa).

Underwood attended Yale University and again Steve Swallow was a fellow student. They regularly travelled to Greenwich Village to hear Ornette Coleman, who became a major influence on Underwood. He graduated from Yale in 1961 with a BA in composition. Swallow went on to become an eminent bassist, working with Paul Bley, Jimmy Giuffre, Stan Getz and Gary Burton, among others.

After Yale, Underwood moved to San Francisco and spent some time gigging with a band called the Jazz Mice. He attempted to follow his parents' advice and studied electrical engineering and mathematics, but music drew him back. In 1967 he graduated from the University of California, Berkeley, with a Masters in Composition, and in the August of that year he was staying with his sister in Manhattan. He accompanied her to the Garrick Theatre to see the Mothers and 'the moment I heard them ... I knew Zappa's music was the closest thing to what really interested me then ...' He met Zappa at Apostolic Studios, where *We're Only in it For the Money* was being recorded, and the story of his recruitment can be heard on the album *Uncle Meat* (1969). He admitted that 'playing with Frank was my first contact with the real world of music, outside of the schools.' Bunk Gardner felt that 'Ian was an excellent musician who never really fit in with the band. He tried real hard to be one of the guys but never succeeded.' And Don Preston said 'I think he felt more comfortable around Frank than anybody else ... I think he might have felt Zappa was more on equal terms than the rest of us who were all under-earners and lowlifes (laughs)' (James, 2001).

The next recruit to the Mothers, in November 1967, was

another musician with jazz inclinations. Art Tripp (born on 10th September 1944 in Athens, Ohio) recounted his story in an interview with Alec Lindsell in 2008. A virtuoso all-round percussionist, he began playing snare drum around the age of ten while at school, and after lessons with Stanley Leonard, a Pittsburgh Symphony Orchestra timpanist, he learned to play xylophone, marimba, timpani, bells and other percussion. In 1961 he enrolled at the Cincinnati Conservatory of Music for the degree of Bachelor of Music, and also became a member of the Cincinnati Symphony Orchestra, performing with artists such as Igor Stravinsky. In 1966 he went on a ten-week world tour with the orchestra, and worked with John Cage when the latter was composer-in-residence at the Cincinnati Conservatory. Having gained his Bachelor's degree in 1966, Tripp began to study for a Master's degree at the Manhattan School of Music in New York, where he was taught by Fred Hinger, one of the all-time great timpanists. A friendship between Tripp's wife and the wife of Dick Kunc, engineer at Apostolic Studios, led to Tripp being introduced to Frank Zappa, who was immediately impressed with his playing. Tripp stated that 'I liked modern jazz … plus, I liked to play free-form.' Though he had no previous experience of rock and roll, his exceptional ability allowed him to fit easily into the Mothers' music and to add an extra dimension to it.

Tripp's initiation into the Mothers included participation in the recording of the album *Uncle Meat*, which took place between October 1967 and May 1968. On this album he shared percussion duties with Ruth Komanoff (later Mrs. Ian Underwood) as well as playing drums. In 1979, when

Dan Forte asked Frank Zappa if *Uncle Meat* was influenced by jazz, Zappa replied 'I don't think there are jazz influences in *Uncle Meat*. If there's any influence in *Uncle Meat* it's from Conlon Nancarrow.' Again, Zappa was being disingenuous: although, as Ben Watson (1994) commented, the album was influential in providing the basis for European art-rock, there was also a strong jazz influence, manifested specifically on the track 'King Kong'. This piece, previewed on the album *Lumpy Gravy*, is a suite, over eighteen minutes in length, made up of six sections seamlessly joined together. As previously mentioned, Ed Palermo (2007) referred to it as 'a modal masterpiece' that proved that Zappa 'had listened to and digested a lot of Miles and Trane.' After the statement of the theme, which in some ways evokes the spirit of Charles Mingus's 'Better Git It In Your Soul' (1959), there follows a series of jazz solos, the first of which is a thoughtful, probing piano excursion by Don Preston. Next comes a frantic free-form baritone sax solo by Motorhead Sherwood, and then Bunk Gardner plays a long, abrasive improvisation on clarinet through an electronic device known as a Maestro box (James, 2001). Throughout, Zappa plays very jazzy rhythm guitar, reminiscent of his work on 'Waltz', which he recorded in 1963 at Pal Studio. He also evokes something of the spirit of guitarist Ray Crawford, as exemplified by his work on the track 'La Nevada' on the Gil Evans album *Out of the Cool* (1960). Section six of 'King Kong' was recorded live at the Miami Pop Festival in May 1968, and is referred to as 'The Underwood Ramifications'. Here, Ian Underwood plays a frenzied alto sax solo that suggests the influence of Albert Ayler, typified by the latter's album *Vibrations* (1964).

Underwood plays a similar solo on 'Ian Underwood Whips It Out', from another version of 'King Kong' recorded live in Copenhagen in October 1967. The 'King Kong' suite is powered throughout by the Elvin Jones-inspired drumming of Art Tripp, who brings things to a climax with a Jones-type drum solo.

CHAPTER 11

BUZZ GARDNER, BURNT WEENY SANDWICH AND WEASELS RIPPED MY FLESH

In November 1968 yet another musician with a strong jazz background joined the Mothers. This was trumpeter Buzz Gardner, brother of Bunk. Born in 1931, he took up trumpet aged seven and heard the big band jazz of Harry James, Tommy Dorsey and Count Basie on the radio and records. In his mid-teens he heard the modern jazz of Dizzy Gillespie and Miles Davis. Around this time he formed a big band with brother Bunk to play local dances, and later studied at Mannes School of Music in New York. From 1951 to 1953 he served in the army and, based in Trieste, he shared a room with future fellow-Mother Don Preston. Between 1954 and 1955 Gardner lived in Paris, studying at the Conservatory of Music and working with a number of eminent French and Belgian jazz musicians. In 1954 he participated in four recordings, one with guitarist René Thomas, one with composer/arranger André Hodeir, and two with tenor saxophonist Bobby Jaspar. The music on all these recordings is excellent, comparing favourably to American jazz of the period, and Gardner shows himself to be a very good modern jazz player who has

45

listened to Miles Davis, Chet Baker and Clifford Brown. Between 1955 and 1959 he was in New York, where he gained a BA from the Manhattan School of Music and, according to the *Zappalog* (2nd edition) of Norbert Obermans, played with the jazz orchestras of Neil Hefti and Claude Thornhill. 1959 saw him moving to Los Angeles with brother Bunk, playing in Latin and jazz groups without a particularly high profile. This was unfortunate, considering his ability as a jazz soloist.

Buzz Gardner joined the Mothers in time to appear on certain tracks on the album *Burnt Weeny Sandwich*, which was recorded between 1967 and 1969, but was not released until 1970. One of the tracks on this album, 'Little House I Used to Live In', is another of Zappa's multi-sectioned works, and is interesting in that it suggested a number of avenues that could be pursued by musicians moving into jazz-rock fusion in the 1970s – avenues that were alternatives to those of Weather Report, The Brecker Brothers, Chick Corea and others. The suite commences with a solo piano piece played by Ian Underwood which, as Ulrik Volgsten (1999) comments, is reminiscent of 'Voiles', one of Claude Debussy's *Preludes*. Strangely, there is also a passing resemblance to Bix Beiderbecke's Debussy-inspired 1927 piano piece 'In a Mist'. Was Zappa a closet Beiderbecke fan? This seems a ludicrous suggestion, yet his 1961 piece, 'High Steppin'', is also Beiderbecke-esque. Section two, which lasts from 1:43 to 4:17, erupts excitingly with the full band and contains three sprightly alternating themes, one of which is in 11/8. This section also appears with the title 'Return of the Hunchback Duke' on *You Can't Do That On Stage Anymore*

Volume 5. Section three, from 4:18 to 5:12 features a short joint improvisation by Zappa on wah-wah guitar and Art Tripp on drums. Section four, lasting from 5:13 to 13:34, is the longest in the suite and is basically a showcase for the intense, impassioned virtuoso blues violin of Sugarcane Harris, playing over a modal vamp. Harris's work here, along with that of Jerry Goodman in the contemporaneous band Flock, paved the way for the violin in a jazz-rock context, as exemplified later by Goodman in Mahavishnu Orchestra. In this section there is also a piano solo by Don Preston which nods to both Dave Brubeck and Cecil Taylor. Section five, lasting from 13:35 to 14:53, is a haunting piece of chamber music featuring trumpet, woodwinds, harpsichord, guitar and vibraphone. Interestingly, whether Zappa was aware of it or not, this section bears a certain resemblance to a piece of Third Stream music composed and recorded by the jazz arranger Johnny Richards in 1955, with a similar instrumentation, entitled *Annotations of the Muses*. In his own way, Zappa took his place in a line of jazz-classical crossover musicians. In fact, in a 1970 interview with Jay Ruby, he acknowledged a parallel between what he was doing and the 1950s Third Stream experiments of Gunther Schuller and John Lewis. 'Little House I Used to Live In' is brought to a close by a section which, unusually, features Zappa playing an organ solo, and more Elvin Jones-inspired drumming by Art Tripp.

The last album by the original Mothers to be released at this time was *Weasels Ripped My Flesh* (1970). Again, there are numerous references to avant-garde jazz, with Albert Ayler-inspired alto sax solos by Ian Underwood appearing on the tracks 'Didja Get Any Onya', 'Prelude to the Afternoon of a Sexually Aroused Gas Mask' and Part Two of 'Toads of the Short Forest'. Art Tripp's jazz chops are evident throughout. There is an interesting moment at 1:40 on 'Didja' when the band breaks into a swinging double tempo section reminiscent of the one on 'How Did That Get in Here?' on *Lumpy Money* (2009). Having admitted his liking for Eric Dolphy on the sleeve of *Freak Out* (1966), Zappa dedicated 'The Eric Dolphy Memorial Barbecue' to him on *Weasels Ripped My Flesh*, and this is possibly the most interesting piece on the album. The melancholy, ominous and tortuously winding theme, with its progressive rhythmic augmentation (Clement, 2009), captures the essence of Dolphy tunes like 'Hat and Beard' and 'Out to Lunch', from the album of the same name (1964) while remaining uniquely Zappa-esque. The vibraphone and synthesiser initially playing the theme in unison pay tribute to Dolphy's band-mate on *Out to Lunch*, vibraphonist Bobby Hutcherson. The jazz possibilities of 'Memorial Barbecue' were extended even further by Zappa's 1988 band, and there is a version on *The Best Band You Never Heard in Your Life* (1991) featuring fine solos by Walt Fowler (sounding not unlike Freddie Hubbard on *Out to Lunch*), Albert Wing, Paul Carman, Chad Wackerman and Ed Mann. Ben Watson, speaking on *The Freak Out List* DVD (Tom O'Dell, 2009), says:

> I found that Dolphy's *Out to Lunch* was the blueprint for all sorts of musical events happening in Zappa. If you explore *Out to Lunch*, you find that Dolphy is listening to

avant-garde classical music, he's thinking in abstract terms
… we're in the same realm of modern music. He [Zappa]
had heroes in jazz – he loved Mingus, he loved Dolphy,
he loved these people and he learned from them.

(O'Dell 2009)

CHAPTER 12

THE MUSIC OF UNEMPLOYMENT

On a number of occasions, well-known jazz musicians either sat in with or played on the same bill as the Mothers. For instance, trumpeter Don Cherry was a guest on 3rd October 1968 at the Tivoli Gardens, Copenhagen (Russo, 2003). Of special interest in this regard is the Boston Globe Jazz Festival, organized by promoter George Wein, which took place on 31st January and 1st February 1969 and featured Dave Brubeck with Gerry Mulligan, Hugh Masakela, Sun Ra and Nina Simone. According to Alan Heineman in the May, 1969 edition of *Downbeat* magazine, the Festival 'offered only one outstanding success in its three concerts.' This was the one that featured the Roland Kirk Quartet and the Mothers of Invention. First of all 'Kirk broke it up' with his quartet and then the final 45 minutes were 'quite literally indescribable.' After the Mothers 'started very free' they 'settled into a jazz framework' and then 'pandemonium broke loose as Kirk wandered out and jammed with them for the rest of the night. All stops were out; Kirk wailed, the Mothers dug it and responded with uncanny support ... Zappa instantly picking up Kirk's concepts and playing telepathic guitar counterpoint ... the audience was close to berserk.' Heineman concluded that 'Kirk and Zappa are crazy if they don't make a record together … An incredible, exhilarating, exhausting, exciting set.' So here was the supposedly jazz-hating Zappa, playing at a jazz festival, jamming with one of his jazz heroes, and being the hit of the concert. George Wein next organized a short East Coast tour featuring a jazz package that comprised the Mothers of Invention, Roland Kirk, the Gary Burton Quartet, and the Duke Ellington Orchestra. The package played the Coliseum, Charlotte, North Carolina as part of the Charlotte Jazz Festival on 28th June, Jai Alai Fronton, Miami, Florida on 29th June and the Newport Jazz Festival, Newport, Rhode Island on 5th July 1969. No doubt Ian Underwood renewed his acquaintance with Steve Swallow, who was playing bass with Gary Burton.

In *The Real Frank Zappa Book* Zappa recounts a story, in relation to the Charlotte, North Carolina Festival, with the heading 'Jazz: The Music of Unemployment'. He says

> Before we went on, I saw Duke Ellington begging – pleading – for a ten-dollar advance. It was really depressing. After the show, I told the guys: "*That's it – we're breaking the band up.*" … suddenly EVERYTHING looked utterly hopeless to me. If Duke Ellington had to beg some George Wein assistant backstage for *ten bucks*, what the fuck was I doing with a ten-piece band, trying to play rock and roll …
>
> *(Zappa 1989, 107)*

Zappa gave a similar version of this story to Neil Slaven, which is quoted in the latter's 1996 book: 'Here's Duke

Ellington, after all these years in the business … begging
the road manager of the tour for a $10 advance. And the
guy wouldn't give it to him. That's like a glimpse into the
future.'

Zappa was attempting to suggest that if the great Duke
Ellington, after a forty five-year career, was still struggling
for money, what chance did he, Zappa, have? As Terry
Teachout (2013) describes, it is true that Ellington had
serious financial problems at the end of his life. When he
died in 1974 it was estimated that he owed between $600,000
and $700,000 in back taxes, and the copyrights to his songs
had to be sold to pay the bills. His son Mercer said that at
his death '… basically he had about three possessions.' Yet
Ellington, one of the key figures in jazz, had enjoyed a
steadily increasing resurgence in popularity, following a
hiatus, after his successful appearance at the Newport Jazz
Festival in 1956. As James Lincoln Collier (1987) recounts,
he won the Presidential Medal of Freedom in 1969, was
being awarded honorary degrees, and was winning polls and
Grammys. Tributes were flooding in. He regularly made long
tours abroad, for instance Japan in 1964, North Africa in
1966, Latin America in 1968 and Eastern Europe in 1969.
As a result his international fame and his prestige in the
United States increased. But Ellington brought his financial
problems upon himself: he was a profligate spender who, as
Terry Teachout states, did not want to operate in a
conventional way. He paid his band members high salaries
and preferred to receive his money in advance so that he
could support himself, his family and his friends in the most
lavish way. For instance, when he was on tour in Russia in

1971 he arranged for steaks that he ate to be shipped directly from New York to Russia via Pan Am airlines.

Jazz did not *have* to be the music of unemployment, as is demonstrated by the lives of other eminent bandleaders. Count Basie died a wealthy man in 1984, as Albert Murray (1985) describes, and Stan Kenton, at his death in 1979, left around $500,000 and his Creative World organization, according to Michael Sparke (2010). But Zappa put a spin on his Ellington story to give the wrong impression, as a reason for breaking up the Mothers. This modus operandi is not unlike the way he regularly put a spin on how he felt about jazz. It is interesting to note that, among Zappa biographers and interviewers, only Barry Miles (2004) questioned the plausibility of this story. Writers and fans generally seemed happy to believe everything Zappa said, while revealing the lack of cross-fertilization of knowledge between the areas of rock and jazz. A further example of Zappa's imaginative interpretation of facts occurred when Neil Slaven asked him whether the Mothers were able to perform his music effectively. He replied: 'They could barely perform it at all. Not only that, when they did perform it, they didn't want to perform it.' This was unjust: the Gardner brothers, Ian Underwood, Don Preston and Art Tripp all read music and between them had several music degrees. But Zappa had new plans. He needed reasons to break up the band and move on.

CHAPTER 13

HOT RATS

During July and August 1969 Zappa recorded *Hot Rats*. This was essentially a joint project with Ian Underwood, and was a sophisticated exercise in overdubbing in which Underwood's layered reeds, woodwinds and keyboards created strange, unusual and highly original orchestral textures. It has often been stated in writings on Zappa that *Hot Rats* is an important, if not the first, jazz-rock album (see, for instance Barry Miles, 2004), and much has been made of the fact that it was recorded around the same time as Miles Davis's *Bitches Brew*. In many ways these observations tend to be simplistic and there is a need for clarification regarding what the jazz influences were in *Hot Rats*, and how it fits into the jazz-rock canon. Many writers, for instance Stuart Nicholson (1998), have tended to emphasize the jazz-rock that developed from 1969 onwards, but this is to ignore the fact that jazz had interacted regularly with rock and roll since the emergence of the latter in the mid-1950s (see Wills, 2009). Arguably, the first jazz-rock recording, in 1958, was Ray Anthony's version of Henry Mancini's 'Peter Gunn' theme. Others, out of many that followed, included 'Beat For Beatniks' by John Barry (1960),

'Image' by Hank Levine (1961), and 'One Mint Julep' by Ray Charles (1961). Jazz-rock went back a long way and was extremely diverse in its presentation. In the late 1960s, the much-maligned Blood, Sweat and Tears actually achieved a convincing blend of jazz and rock influences via the arrangements of Dick Halligan and the excellent solo abilities of Lew Soloff, Fred Lipsius and Bobby Colomby. In the next wave of jazz-rock that arrived, featuring Miles Davis spinoffs Weather Report, Mahavishnu Orchestra and Return To Forever, also the New York-based sound which filtered through the bands White Elephant, Dreams and the Brecker Brothers, and the West Coast-based music of The Crusaders and Tom Scott, *Hot Rats* was an anomaly, a one-off phenomenon. Greatly admired by both jazz and rock musicians, essentially it showed how jazz chops and innovative production techniques could contribute in subtle and complex ways to rock. As Richard Bock, founder of Pacific Jazz Records, said to Leonard Feather in 1970, it 'was hard to classify; just fascinating instrumental music.'

Whereas the original Mothers could sound at times like a lumbering juggernaut with their two-drummer team, on *Hot Rats* Zappa created a new dimension in his music by using a different type of rhythm section. The drummers, Ron Selico, Paul Humphrey and John Guerin, were all jazz musicians who were also masters in the fields of rhythm and blues and/or funk drumming. Ron Selico, after playing hard bop with the legendary trumpeter Dupree Bolton in Curtis Amy's group, had developed his funk chops with James Brown and had played with Shuggie Otis in Preston Love's rhythm and blues group. Paul Humphrey had played jazz with the Montgomery Brothers, Les McCann, Joe Pass and Blue Mitchell, and blues with Otis Spann and T-Bone Walker. John Guerin (31st October 1939 – 5th January 2004) made a crucial contribution to *Hot Rats*. He had first worked with Zappa on the *Run Home Slow* soundtrack (1963) and then on *Lumpy Gravy* (1968). Starting his career playing straight-ahead jazz with Buddy DeFranco and George Shearing, he later became one of the great jazz-rock drummers, with a style as distinctive in its own way as that of his peers Billy Cobham, Steve Gadd and Harvey Mason. The Guerin style featured tasty fills around his single-head concert tom toms, displaced accents, and the frequent playing of 3/4 against 4/4/. Bassist Max Bennett, aged forty one at the time of recording *Hot Rats*, was a veteran of the 1950s West Coast jazz scene and had played with the Stan Kenton orchestra. An open-minded and forward-thinking musician, he started to appreciate the possibilities of rock when he became involved in recording sessions. And the importance of rhythm and blues father-figure Johnny Otis in the creation of *Hot Rats* cannot be over-estimated: he helped Zappa locate Sugarcane Harris (who, as Barry Miles (2004) reports, was in jail at the time) for the sessions, and his son Shuggie played bass on 'Peaches en Regalia'.

The music on *Hot Rats* manages to seamlessly encompass the widely-differing styles of sophisticated rhythm and blues, surreal, cartoon-esque and compelling soundscapes, and electric chamber music. Into the latter category fall 'Little Umbrellas' and 'It Must Be a Camel', both featuring Max Bennett on bass and John Guerin on drums. 'Little Umbrellas', a feature for Ian Underwood's reeds and keyboards, has a lugubrious theme, stated by a soprano-led saxophone section, that nods to the 'Funeral March' movement from Chopin's B-flat Minor Piano Sonata. Keyboards follow, with lines that would have been at home on *Uncle Meat*. Everything is solidly underpinned by Bennett's double bass and the trademark sound of Guerin's drums. 'It Must Be a Camel', in 3/4, has a convoluted theme reminiscent of 'The Eric Dolphy Memorial Barbecue'. A central section in 4/4, featuring a plangent Zappa guitar solo, is led back into the theme by an archetypal John Guerin drum fill, played on his concert toms. On 'Willie the Pimp', Bennett and Guerin dazzle in a different way as they demonstrate the telepathic interplay that would later become a trademark of their teamwork with Tom Scott and the LA Express (1973, 1974). As Zappa plays a classic blues-rock guitar solo that builds relentlessly to a climax of almost unbearable intensity, Bennett and Guerin lay down a solid groove that both rocks and swings. Gradually Guerin increases the complexity of his drum fills, starting to displace accents while Bennett empathically catches each one. At 6:30 they switch into double time and then at 8:00 a solid four-in-a-bar builds to three against four, and everyone tumbles back into the theme.

The most straightforwardly funky track on *Hot Rats* is 'The Gumbo Variations'. One has the impression that Ian Underwood had been listening to one of Albert Ayler's excursions into funk: namely the track 'New Generation', from his album *New Grass* (1968). 'The Gumbo Variations' is not unlike a slowed-down version of 'New Generation', with a similar funk bass line, and Underwood's raucous tenor solo closely resembles Ayler's. Everything is underpinned by a John Patton-like organ riff. Underwood is followed by the hot virtuoso blues violin of Sugarcane Harris and the track is driven by the fantastically tight rhythm section of Max Bennett and Paul Humphrey, picking up figures together and pushing the music along with exciting fills. Humphrey's funk drumming is in the same league as that of Bernard Purdie and Clyde Stubblefield. When Zappa enters with his guitar solo, Humphrey embarks on a duet with him, urging him on. As Zappa's solo finishes, Humphrey plays a four-bar break that is a classic of funk drumming, and then duets with Max Bennett for eight bars. The track finishes with the re-entry of Sugar Cane Harris.

'Son of Mr. Green Genes' brings together all the disparate qualities of *Hot Rats* in one track: majestic orchestral sounds and cartoon-esque humour created by Underwood's reeds and keyboards, fitting perfectly with Zappa's urgently fluent guitar and a funky rhythm section. 'Peaches en Regalia' is probably Zappa's best known composition. It has a majestic, imperious quality: by turns gothic, anthemic and mischievous, it flows through a series of sections, each with a unique combination of melody, harmony, instrumentation and rhythm. As Ted Gioia (2009) has stated, 'it could serve as the soundtrack for the coronation of a mad king.' Jazz musicians seem to have a special affection for 'Peaches en Regalia', and why this should be so is, to quote Gioia again, '…a bit of a mystery … 'Peaches en Regalia' is one of those crazy, complicated Zappa tunes that is not your typical jam session fare.' As has been stated, *Hot Rats* is not a jazz-rock album in the conventional sense, but its outstanding musicianship gave jazz and rock musicians the inspiration to play rock and crossover music in a new way. It did not give birth to a new genre in the way that the music of Weather Report, Mahavishnu Orchestra or Chick Corea did. On *The Freak Out List* DVD (2009), Stuart Nicholson says, 'To me it is probably *the* most effective combination of jazz and rock for that time, 1969.' However, it was not as simple as that: Zappa took the skills of jazz musicians and subverted them for his own reasons.

The track 'Twenty Small Cigars' was recorded at the *Hot Rats* sessions, but appeared on the later album *Chunga's Revenge* (1970). Yet another of Zappa's jazz waltzes, it is languid and insinuating, and the melody line bears a certain resemblance to Thelonious Monk's 'Round Midnight', as Beppe Colli (2012) has remarked. It features Zappa on both guitar and harpsichord, accompanied by Underwood, Bennett and Guerin. Versions by Riccardo Fassi (1994) and Ed Palermo (1997) have highlighted its strong jazz underpinnings.

CHAPTER 14

KING KONG

It was at the time that *Hot Rats* was being recorded that Zappa became acquainted with jazz violinist Jean-Luc Ponty (born 29th September 1942). The catalyst for this meeting was Richard Bock (1927-1988), who was one of the most significant figures in West Coast jazz. In 1952 he had founded the Pacific Jazz label in order to record the classic Gerry Mulligan Quartet with Chet Baker, and he went on to record numerous other musicians such as Art Pepper, Jim Hall, Wes Montgomery, Les McCann, Paul Desmond, Joe Pass and Gerald Wilson. In 1958 he founded the World Pacific label. Having become aware of Jean-Luc Ponty when the latter played at the Monterey Jazz Festival in 1967, Bock contacted him in 1968 and signed him to his Pacific Jazz label, as Ponty told Mark Gilbert in 1997. Meanwhile, pianist George Duke had heard a Ponty record on the radio and, feeling that he would be the perfect musical companion for Ponty, he sent a tape to Richard Bock. Duke (12th January 1946 – 5th August 2013) had gained a B. Mus. in composition from San Francisco Conservatory, and he worked with his trio in San Francisco, accompanying jazz stars like Dizzy Gillespie, Bobby Hutcherson and Kenny Dorham. In 1969

Bock produced three albums for Ponty, and Duke was the pianist on all three. The first was *Electric Connection*, with the Gerald Wilson Orchestra, followed by *Live at Donte's* and *The Jean-Luc Ponty Experience*. Duke's trio accompanied Ponty on the latter two. Richard Bock was always on the lookout for new music – he had recorded Ravi Shankar in 1962 – and, as he said to Leonard Feather in 1970, he had heard more and more about Frank Zappa in jazz circles. He visited Zappa at a *Hot Rats* recording session, and then took an acetate of Ponty to Zappa's house. Impressed by what he heard, Zappa went to see Ponty playing with the George Duke Trio at Thee Experience, a Los Angeles rock club where his third album for Bock was recorded, and where he was creating such a sensation that luminaries such as Quincy Jones and Cannonball Adderley were appearing in the audience. Zappa sat in with Ponty: as George Duke described it to Steve Metalitz (*Downbeat*, November 7, 1974), 'He asked if he could play. He came up and jammed a blues.' As a result, Ponty featured briefly on the *Hot Rats* track 'It Must Be a Camel'. Bock, who wanted to make a commercial record with Ponty, had initially suggested recording an album of tunes by The Doors or Fifth Dimension, but Ponty refused and so the idea was formulated that he would record an album arranged and overseen by Zappa.

King Kong: Jean-Luc Ponty Plays the Music of Frank Zappa was recorded at three sessions in October, 1969. Two separate basic groups were used for the sessions, but George Duke was common to both. One group contained Zappa's now-familiar colleague John Guerin, along with saxophonist Ernie Watts (born 23rd October 1945) and bassist Wilton

Felder (born 31ˢᵗ August 1940). Watts, a Berklee graduate and Buddy Rich alumnus, would work with Zappa again on the *Grand Wazoo* album. Felder, tenor saxophonist with The Jazz Crusaders, had also branched out into sessions playing bass. The rhythm section of the other group comprised ex-Mother Art Tripp on drums, and Buell Neidlinger as bass player. Neidlinger (born 2ⁿᵈ March 1936) was one of the earliest free jazz bassists and appeared on recordings by Cecil Taylor, Archie Shepp, Steve Lacy and Jimmy Giuffre. At the time of the Ponty recording he was with the Boston Symphony Orchestra. In an Alan Heineman *Downbeat* 1972 Yearbook interview he said, '… Frank knew my work from Cecil's recordings, and I knew Ian Underwood from when I went to Yale …' There had been some talk of Neidlinger joining The Mothers:

> Then he called later and asked me to record with Jean-Luc Ponty … I flew out there and made these sessions with him. Got tight. Stayed over at his house and had a lot of fun together, played a lot of music.
>
> *(Heineman 1972, 13)*

In a 2003 interview with Clifford Allen for *All About Jazz*, he described the stay at Zappa's house as

> a turning point in my life. That day I met Mel Powell, who was the dean of music at the new school and had been interested in hiring me. After our meeting in Frank's basement he hired me and I went to Cal Arts.
>
> *(Allen 2003, 5)*

Prior to being a music educator and atonal composer, Mel Powell had been a virtuoso jazz pianist, working as a teenager with Benny Goodman and, later, Glenn Miller. It is fascinating to consider how many individuals with jazz connections, like Richard Bock (purveyor of that 'bleak' West Coast jazz), Buell Neidlinger and Mel Powell, congregated at one time or another in Zappa's basement, although Zappa did not broadcast the fact. Even Leonard Feather, dean of jazz critics, interviewed him in order to write sleeve notes for the Ponty album. And, according to eminent jazz writer Ira Gitler (1982), Allen Eager, one of the premier 'cool' bebop tenor sax players of the late 1940s and early 1950s, 'In the '70s ... was living in California, playing soprano and sitting in on occasion with The Mothers of Invention'. Ironically, as mentioned previously, when Bunk Gardner joined Zappa in 1966, he was persuaded to stop playing in the style that Eager used.

Although *King Kong* is nominally Ponty's album, it is really Zappa's. The next step on in his musical development, it is more of a jazz-rock album than *Hot Rats*, as well as containing strong elements of mainstream jazz and a large portion of Third Stream music. The excellent piano of George Duke, both acoustic and electric, lays down a solid jazz bedrock for the album, not only in the rhythm sections but also in funk- and blues-inflected solos that reflect the influences of Les McCann, Herbie Hancock and McCoy Tyner. With Duke behind him, Ponty plays a searing, virtuoso violin inspired by Stephane Grappelli, Stuff Smith and John Coltrane. The album's tour de force is 'Music for Electric Violin and Low Budget Orchestra', a suite, played by a ten-piece chamber group, that is over nineteen minutes long and is divided into five sections. The first part reflects the influence of Stravinsky on Zappa, and there is a hint of the former's 'Concertino for 12 Instruments'. Part two is a slow jazz version of 'Duke of Prunes', featuring a Hancock/Tyner-influenced solo by Duke. Parts three and four feature dissonant orchestral music similar to sections of *Lumpy Gravy*, and part four also includes another Albert Ayler-influenced tenor sax solo by Ian Underwood. The suite is completed by a version of 'A Pound for a Brown'. A tight, exciting version of 'King Kong' sees Ponty backed by Ian Underwood's tenor sax plus a swinging rhythm section of piano, vibes, bass and drums. This version of the tune undoubtedly introduced its jazz possibilities to the world at large. 'How Would You Like to Have a Head Like That', composed by Ponty, is more straightforwardly jazz-rock fusion than anything on *Hot Rats*, and both Ernie Watts and Zappa play fluent solos over Wilton Felder's funky bass line. 'Idiot Bastard Son' and 'Twenty Small Cigars' provide further demonstrations of Zappa's propensity for the jazz waltz. *King Kong* marked Zappa's introduction to Ponty and Duke, both of whom would make significant reappearances in his music. Duke would continue to inject a strong personal note until the mid-1970s. Richard Bock, Buell Neidlinger and Ernie Watts all created jazz input.

CHAPTER 15

AMOUGIES AND THE LA PHILHARMONIC

After completing the recording of *King Kong*, Zappa travelled to Europe in order to fulfil two overlapping roles: the first was as road manager for Captain Beefheart and the Magic Band on their European tour, and the second was as Master of Ceremonies at the Actuel Festival in Amougies, Belgium, which ran from the 24th to the 28th October 1969. As Jane Welch, in a 1970 *Downbeat* report, said, 'The festival was a daring project from the start,' because the music presented was a mixture of rock, free jazz and new music. The cream of British progressive rock bands appeared, including Ten Years After, Colosseum, The Aynsley Dunbar Retaliation, Pink Floyd, The Nice, Caravan, Blossom Toes, Yes and The Pretty Things. The free jazz contingent included The Art Ensemble of Chicago, Sunny Murray, Grachan Moncur III, Don Cherry, Archie Shepp, Anthony Braxton and Pharoah Sanders. As well as acting as Master of Ceremonies and introducing Captain Beefheart, Zappa sat in with several bands, including Pink Floyd. Strangely, in a 1990 interview with Den Simms in *Society Pages* magazine, he denied playing with Floyd, even though bootleg recordings and photographs of the event exist, as reported by Scott Parker

(2007). Again, Zappa was exhibiting his own unique interpretation of a situation. Most interestingly from a jazz point of view, he sat in with a group of free musicians that included Archie Shepp, trombonist Grachan Moncur III, bassists Earl Freeman and Johnny Dyani and drummers Philly Joe Jones and Louis Moholo. According to Jane Welch (1970), 'Zappa listened to the avant garde jazz with the same rapt interest as to the rock, and even with childlike innocence sat in with Archie Shepp's group ... Frank befriended many jazz musicians.'

It is intriguing to consider that, despite the anti-Establishment image that he projected, Zappa associated closely with many eminent Establishment figures. As has been mentioned, he was a good friend of David Raksin, who wrote the classic scores for the movies *Laura* (1944), *Forever Amber* (1947) and *The Bad and the Beautiful* (1952). As David Walley (1996) discusses, Raksin was a professor at the University of Southern California (USC), where he ran a class called the Urban Semester. Zappa had been a guest at the class along with Randy Newman (whose uncles, Alfred and Lionel, were also eminent film composers) and Henry Mancini. Soon after, Raksin brought Zappa into a panel discussion about music that took place on the radio station KPFK early in 1970. As Gordon Skene (2011) reports, it can be heard at the *Crooks and Liars* website. The other panel members included Zubin Mehta, conductor of the Los Angeles Philharmonic, and Ernest Fleischmann, the Philharmonic manager. Zappa fitted smoothly into the discussion, and his meeting with Mehta led to a live performance of his orchestral work '200 Motels' by a reformed version of The Mothers and the Los Angeles Philharmonic in May 1970. Zappa discussed how he met Mehta, and his preparations for the concert with him, in an interview with Jay Ruby in 1970. He also mentioned the names of some of the musicians who would be appearing with the orchestra: Emil Richards, John Rotella, Ernie Watts and George Duke. He said:

> Emil Richards is joining the percussion section. I've got to go over to his house because he's got that exotic collection of gongs and weirdness … This other guy that I worked with, and who I like very much is John Rotella. He's going to be playing the baritone and bass sax parts, and Ernie Watts is playing the alto and tenor part of the orchestra … I've got one more added attraction – do you know George Duke? He's going to be playing the celeste and electric piano part with the orchestra. I like his playing very much.
>
> *(Ruby 1970, 20)*

First-class jazz and session musicians continued to play an intrinsic part in Zappa's work on a personal and professional level.

In a September, 1970, edition of *Strange Days* magazine, in an article by Chris Hodenfield about Zappa, he was quoted as saying that he liked the Miles Davis album *Nefertiti*. He felt that it was 'good because it was free, but not crazed.' This was an interesting admission that contradicted his previously-mentioned later statement, in the 1984 *RockBill* magazine, that he had not had anything to do with Davis or his music since 1961.

CHAPTER 16

WAKA/JAWAKA AND THE GRAND WAZOO

On 10th December 1971 Zappa was pushed off stage by a fan while playing at the Rainbow Theatre in London. He spent the next four months with a leg in plaster up to the hip, but, though physically immobilized, he plunged into new writing projects, including the creation of two long musical works, 'Hunchentoot' and 'The Adventures of Greggery Peccary'. In the meantime, his band was kept on hold, possibly because he was displeased with them: singers Howard Kaylan and Mark Volman, as they reported to Co de Kloet in *Society Pages 11* (1992), had joked to the press that Zappa had jumped off stage at the Rainbow Theatre, rather than being pushed.

Zappa's main focus throughout April and May 1972 was the recording of material for the albums *Waka/Jawaka* and *The Grand Wazoo*. Essentially, the instrumental material on these albums was a continuation of certain aspects of the *Lumpy Gravy* era, as exemplified by sections of the tracks 'How Did That Get In Here?', and 'Section 8, Take 22' on *The Lumpy Money Project/Object* (2009) – orchestral music with a jazz-rock feel. In fact, Zappa was quoted in the December

1971 Rainbow Theatre Programme as saying 'I intend to keep on writing things for orchestras.' Also, Barry Miles (2004) suggests that 'lying idle in hospital, Frank had clearly been listening to a lot of jazz fusion.' Musicians assembled for the *Jawaka/Wazoo* sessions displayed a formidable array of jazz credentials: trumpeter Sal Marquez (born 21st December 1943) was an ex-Woody Herman, Buddy Rich and Gerald Wilson sideman, while trombonist Kenny Shroyer, after starting his career with Stan Kenton in 1956, worked with Shorty Rogers, Pete Rugolo, Bill Holman and Gerald Wilson. Reed man Anthony Ortega (born 7th June 1928) was a veteran of the bands of Lionel Hampton, Quincy Jones, Maynard Ferguson and Blue Mitchell. Fellow reed man Mike Altschul (born 27th December 1945) was a member of the orchestras of Stan Kenton from1967 to 1968 (as was Earl Dumler) and Don Ellis (1969). John Rotella and Ernie Watts were already regarded by Zappa as valued colleagues. It was also fascinating to see trombonist and arranger Billy Byers participating in these recordings. Byers (1st May 1927 – 1st May 1996) was a brilliant and respected musician who, in a career commencing in 1949, had worked with nearly everyone of note in the jazz world before settling in the LA studios. Trombonist Bruce Fowler, who was in the live Wazoo bands that followed the recordings under discussion, made some interesting comments regarding Byers in the 2003 Shaar Murray Radio 4 broadcast:

> Billy Byers was in that band, and he was one of the best arrangers in history. And these jazz friends were these arranger guys, and I'm sure they went over to his [Frank's]

house and played him some stuff, or at least he was probably asking people, who could really write a great arrangement? Because, you know, Frank wanted to learn stuff, he's gonna, … need to learn something from a guy like that.

(Shaar Murray 2003, BBC Radio 3)

So it is likely that Zappa was absorbing information from contemporaneous orchestral jazz material. One might surmise that the Don Ellis orchestra was an inspiration for the *Jawaka/Wazoo* albums, but Ellis used fairly conventional big band arrangements: they simply had unusual time signatures (as witness, for instance, his 1971 album *Tears of Joy*). *Waka/Jawaka* and *The Grand Wazoo* sit more comfortably alongside two innovative jazz-rock/Third Stream albums: *America the Beautiful* (1969) by Gary McFarland and *Blues in Orbit* (1971) by Gil Evans. McFarland's music was a comment on a topic close to Zappa's heart – the way that war and corporate greed were undermining the American dream. 20th century classical, orchestral jazz and funk influences were blended with poignancy and wry humour. Evans's album was his first solo effort for five years and it signalled a change in direction after listening to the music of Jimi Hendrix. The inclusion of the George Russell tune 'Blues in Orbit', with its urgent swing-shuffle tempo and string of solos alternating with ensemble sections, in certain ways foreshadowed the title track of *The Grand Wazoo*. It is also interesting to consider Russell here in the context of his Lydian Chromatic Concept of Tonal Organization (1953). Brett Clement (2009) comments that Russell advocates viewing chords and scales as being virtually synonymous. The basis of Russell's theory is that the Lydian scale best represents the sound of the major chord. Clement states that

> Certain aspects of Zappa's music, including the preference for slow harmonic rhythm and improvisatory melody, seem tailor-made for Russell's theories ... Zappa's approach to modality – particularly his preference for the Lydian mode – offers the potential for parallels. In fact, the Lydian mode can be considered the characteristic sound of Zappa's diatonic music.
>
> *(Clement 2009, 116)*

Clement stresses that there is no evidence that Zappa was familiar with the Lydian Chromatic Concept. Nevertheless, it is an intriguing coincidence.

Zappa's rhythm section for the *Jawaka/Wazoo* sessions was Aynsley Dunbar (born 10th January 1946), drummer with the 1970/71 band, and Alex Dmochowski, bassist from Dunbar's band Retaliation. At first glance there seemed something odd about two stalwarts of the late-1960s British blues-rock scene powering a group of ex-Stan Kenton, Woody Herman, Buddy Rich and Shorty Rogers sidemen, but the juxtaposition worked well. In a May, 1982 *Modern Drummer* interview with Rick Mattingly, Dunbar described how '*Grand Wazoo* was charts. Most of the drum parts on that were written down. *Waka/Jawaka* was also a jazz album'. But Zappa allowed him to express himself within the constraints of the drum parts.

The title track of *The Grand Wazoo* is an instrumental

version of the song 'Think It Over', which Zappa had written as part of 'Hunchentoot'. Surging along with a swing-shuffle feel, it moves through five separate themes during its 13:22 length, conjuring, as mentioned, the spirit of Gil Evans's 1969 recording of George Russell's 'Blues In Orbit', and also the track 'Due To Lack of Interest' from Gary McFarland's *America the Beautiful* (1969). Theme five also has a hint of Ernie Wilkins's arrangement of 'Kelly Blue' from the Cannonball Adderley Orchestra's album *African Waltz* (1961). Powerful brass is cushioned by subtle blends of woodwind and tuned percussion, and everything is underpinned by Aynsley Dunbar's drums as he becomes a rock version of Elvin Jones. After the statement of the fifth theme Billy Byers enters with an exemplary jazz trombone solo that is mellow, kicking and fluent. He is followed by Sal Marquez, whose muted wah-wah trumpet solo sounds like a humorous tribute to Cootie Williams. Next, Don Preston, a member of the 1971 Zappa band following a stint with the Gil Evans Orchestra and recording with Carla Bley, plays a burbling, evocative synthesiser solo.

'For Calvin (And His Next Two Hitchhikers)' is a composite piece, starting with a short, bizarre story-song in 3/4 with vocals by Sal Marquez and Janet Neville-Ferguson. Dissonant orchestral music commences at 1:20, and at 2:13 a Don Preston solo suggests how Cecil Taylor might sound playing synthesiser. There follows a trombone duet in which Billy Byers sounds like Tricky Sam Nanton and Kenny Shroyer plays the theme from 'New Brown Clouds', part of 'Greggery Peccary'. Next, more dissonant orchestral music, featuring Zappa's typically convoluted lines, gives the impression that it has been left out of the 'Greggery Peccary' suite that finally appeared on *Studio Tan* in 1978. The piece concludes with a return to the opening theme. This track can definitely *not* be classed as big band jazz-rock.

The same assessment can also be applied to 'Cletus Awreetus-Awrightus', which, with Bavarian oompah band music, honky-tonk tack piano, a sea-sick tenor sax solo by Ernie Watts and silly rum-pum-pum vocals, is cartoon soundtrack music. It includes, and finishes with, a quote from 'Zomby Woof', later to appear on the album *Over-Nite Sensation* (1973).

Comment has already been made in a previous section about 'Blessed Relief'. It is worth repeating that it is an excellent jazz waltz that captures the spirit of Frank Rosolino's tune 'Blue Daniel', and it also has something of the ambience of 'Tell Me a Bedtime Story' from Herbie Hancock's 1970 album *Fat Albert Rotunda*. Working in a medium-sized band setting, Sal Marquez shows his allegiance to the work of Freddie Hubbard, and Zappa, with a gentle, reflective solo, gives evidence of his ability to improvise over an interesting chord sequence.

'Eat That Question' utilizes a theme based on a four-bar riff that acts as a launching pad for solos by George Duke and Zappa. This track provides perhaps the key demonstration of the way in which Duke introduced jazz-funk into Zappa's music. Starting as a straight-ahead jazz pianist, Duke was already forging a solo career in funk and pop with his albums *Save the Country* (1970), and *The Inner Source* (1971), while also having previously been a Zappa band member in 1970-1971. He had absorbed the new jazz-funk directions pioneered by Herbie Hancock on electric piano, first with Miles Davis and later on his own albums like *Fat Albert Rotunda* (1970). At the time of playing on the sessions for the *Jawaka/Wazoo* albums, Duke was a member of the Cannonball Adderley Quintet, and had replaced another pioneer of electric jazz piano, Joe Zawinul. Adderley himself had been moving in a soul-jazz-funk direction with albums like *The Black Messiah* (1971). Duke's solo on 'Eat That Question' is an exciting, virtuoso exercise in jazz-funk piano that compares well with Hancock's work of the same period. It inspires Zappa to enter with an echoing wah-wah guitar solo that invokes the spirit of Jimi Hendrix's 'All Along The Watchtower'. Everything is underpinned by Aynsley Dunbar's increasingly frantic drumming, and the track climaxes with a reiteration of the opening riff augmented by trumpet and reeds.

'Big Swifty' opens with a theme that is derived from part of Zappa's guitar solo on the version of 'King Kong' played in London on 10th December 1971. It is actually part of 'The New Brown Clouds', from the 'Greggery Peccary' suite, as can be heard on a recording of a rehearsal, prior to the *Jawaka/Wazoo* recordings, on the *Joe's Domage* album (2004). The main theme features archetypal Zappa rhythmic complexity: twenty four bars alternating between two bars of 7/8 and two bars of 3/4, eighteen bars where three bars of 5/8 are followed by six bars of 3/4, twice, four bars of 7/8 and, finally, sixteen bars of 4/4. Zappa's guitar trades melody lines with the fanfares of the one-man, multi-tracked, partially-speeded-up trumpet section created by Sal Marquez. The effect is like listening to the brass section of a cartoon big band. The final 4/4 section stomps through a drunken riff and spins downwards into a shimmering haze of percussive and electronic effects, which pay lip service to Miles Davis's *Bitches Brew* (1970). This transition from the opening theme statement to the long section of solos that follows is like Alice in Wonderland falling down the rabbit hole, out of the sunlight into a nether-world. George Duke enters with Herbie Hancock-inflected piano, as Aynsley Dunbar provides a perpetual-motion, triplet-feel shuffle. A mysterious, modal, Moorish mood, somewhere between Miles Davis's *Sketches of Spain* (1960) and Horace Silver's 'Senor Blues' (1956), is evoked. At 3:30, Sal Marquez's solo fades in, reminiscent of Freddie Hubbard on another influential jazz-fusion album, *Red Clay* (1970). A sense of collective improvisation is created, with agitated fragments of guitar and piano worrying Marquez along. At 5:30 Zappa commences his solo, suggesting the flights of fancy of a deranged flamenco guitarist rather than the neurotic, machine-gun precision of John McLaughlin, with whom he was sometimes compared during this period (see, for instance, Neil Slaven, 1996). At 9:30 a 'Grand Wazoo'-style shuffle commences, preparing the way for Tony Duran's slide guitar solo. 'Big Swifty' draws to a close with a slowed-down version of the theme, which, as Zappa said 'suspends the opening rhythmic structure over a straight 4/4 accompaniment.' He continued:

> The restatement of the theme is actually derived from a guitar solo on the album which Sal Marquez took down on paper. After about an hour of wheeling the tape back

and forth, Sal managed to transcribe this rhythmically deranged chorus ... After he'd written it out, we proceeded to overdub three trumpets on it, and, presto! An organized conclusion for 'Big Swifty'.

(Zappa 1972, 3).

For his part, Marquez, in an interview in the February, 1994, *Musician* Magazine, said 'I just sat back and wrote down his licks while he played them, which I suspect he was very impressed with.' Marquez also stated that he wrote and arranged all the horn parts for *Waka/Jawaka* and *The Grand Wazoo*, but one wonders how true this is, considering that Zappa had been writing horn parts for years, for instance on albums like *Freak Out* and *Lumpy Gravy*. Trombonist Glenn Ferris, a member of the live Grand and Petit Wazoos, when interviewed by Christophe Delbrouck in the June 2008 French *Jazz Magazine*, said, 'He [Zappa] knew all the parts. He had written them all and he knew if they could be played or not. He was very sharp.'

The track 'Waka/Jawaka' is a classic example of big-band jazz-rock, albeit with Zappa's unique stamp on it. Ben Watson (1994) is correct when he describes its theme as 'a distant cousin of Ravel's 'Bolero''. The brass section is multi-tracked by Sal Marquez, Billy Byers and Kenny Shroyer, while Mike Altschul, via overdubs, is a one-man reed and woodwind section. Utilizing a medium rock tempo, the lofty, imperious theme, stated by the full orchestra, gives way to a lucid, declamatory, Mariachi-flavoured trumpet solo by Sal Marquez. Next follows a mini-moog solo by Don Preston which, in a 2001 interview with Steve Moore, he rated as his favourite example of his synthesiser work. Zappa's guitar solo opens with what could possibly be construed as an ironic quote from the Jimmy Van Heusen/Sammy Cahn standard 'All The Way', and the ensemble passage which follows, including unison wordless vocals by Sal Marquez and Kris Peterson, sounds as though Zappa might be having a sly dig at Ray Conniff's orchestra and singers (compare it to ''s Wonderful' on Conniff's eponymous 1956 album). At 6:51 Marquez again demonstrates his trumpet virtuosity when he plays in unison with an intricate Zappa guitar line. Throughout, Aynsley Dunbar's drums constantly push and probe, confirming Zappa's opinion, in an interview with Kathy Orloff in 1970, that 'Aynsley has a rhythmic concept that none of my other drummers have had.' At 7:09, a section of shouting big band riffing that might have come from an Ernie Wilkins arrangement sets up an action-packed Dunbar drum solo, featuring ankle-punishing bass drum triplets. A majestic finale follows, complete with chimes that blend with the brass section.

Considerable space has been devoted here to discussing *Waka/Jawaka* and *The Grand Wazoo* because writers on Zappa generally seem to consider these two albums to be most representative of the jazz influences in his work. For instance, Nicholson (1998) describes them as 'two ambitious jazz-rock albums' and Fisher Lowe (2006) feels that 'both albums are essentially big band/jazz fusion albums.' These statements are broadly true, but are also too simplistic and need clarification. Out of nine tracks on the albums, only four ('Big Swifty', 'Waka/Jawaka', 'The Grand Wazoo' and 'Eat That Question') could be described as having big band jazz-rock content and one ('Blessed Relief') is straight-ahead jazz by a medium-sized band. Three of the tracks ('Your Mouth', 'It Just Might Be a One-Shot Deal', and 'Cletus Awreetus-Awrightus') have no jazz content. Writers tend to over-emphasise the influence of Miles Davis on the music: for instance, Fisher Lowe (2006) says that 'most critics cite Miles Davis as the main inspiration for both albums.' But there are many clues and jazz influences in Zappa's previous work that suggest he was heading in the direction of these albums. And at the time, the work of musicians like Gary McFarland, Herbie Hancock and Freddie Hubbard was also in the air. But whatever influences Zappa may have tacitly acknowledged, his music always bore his own unique imprint.

CHAPTER 17

GRAND WAZOO LIVE

After recording *Waka/Jawaka* and *The Grand Wazoo*, Zappa decided to form a live touring orchestra that would play selections from the albums, as well as other music, some of which had not yet been recorded. In an October, 1972, Warner/Reprise circular, he stated:

> Since the earliest days of the M.O.I. (from about 1964, roughly), I have been interested in assembling some kind of electric orchestra, capable of performing intricate compositions of the same sound-intensity levels normally associated with other forms of pop music. The formation of the new MOTHERS OF INVENTION/HOT RATS/ GRAND WAZOO represents the first large-scale attempt to mount such a monstrosity and to actually move it across a couple of continents to do concerts.
>
> *(Zappa 1972, 3)*

In recruiting orchestra members, from the *Jawaka/Wazoo* recording sessions Zappa retained trumpeters Sal Marquez and Malcolm McNab, trombonist Kenny Shroyer and reed players Mike Altschul, Earl Dumler and JoAnn McNab.

Aynsley Dunbar and Alex Dmochowski moved on: according to Mark Volman in his 1992 interview with Co de Kloet, 'Frank had had some negative run-ins with Aynsley' and Dmochowski was unable to obtain a work permit (personal communication with the author, 1993). A new rhythm section contained a returning Ian Underwood on keyboards and his wife Ruth (born 23rd May 1946), in her first experience as a regular Zappa band member, on marimba. Second percussion place was filled by Tom Raney, a graduate of the University of Southern California with wide experience in contemporary music. Dave Parlato (born 31st October 1945), after jazz experience with Don Ellis, Frank Strazzeri, Warne Marsh and Paul Horn, joined on bass. The drum chair was taken by Jim Gordon (born 14th July 1945), who at the time was one of the most in-demand session drummers in the world: his recent credits had included work with Joe Cocker, George Harrison, Derek and the Dominos, Traffic and Harry Nilsson.

There were three new recruits to the brass section. Trumpeter Tom Malone (born 16th June 1947) was an exceptionally versatile musician who, when required, could also play trombone, tuba, euphonium, saxophones and flute. He had previously worked with The Supremes, The Temptations, Marvin Gaye and the jazz orchestras of Woody Herman and Duke Pearson. Trombonist Bruce Fowler (born 10th July 1947) was the son of music educator William Fowler, had been a colleague of Tom Malone at North Texas State University and had also worked with Woody Herman. Fellow trombonist Glenn Ferris (born 27th June 1950) had been a member of the Don Ellis orchestra between 1966 and 1970.

Three new recruits also joined the reed section. Veteran reed player Jay Migliori (born 14th November 1930) had, ironically, led a band on the previously-mentioned Tom Wilson-produced *Jazz in Transition* album that Zappa had discussed with Frank Kofsky in 1967. He had worked with the orchestras of Woody Herman, Charlie Barnet, Si Zentner, Terry Gibbs and Gerald Wilson. Ray Reed (born 19th September 1942) had been a member of the Stan Kenton orchestra and Charles Owens (born 4th May 1939) had jazz experience with Buddy Rich, Mongo Santamaria, Bobby Bryant and Bobby Hutcherson.

The Grand Wazoo Orchestra toured between the 10th and the 24th September 1972, and played dates in Los Angeles, Berlin, London, The Hague, New York and Boston. A recording of the final concert in Boston, entitled *Wazoo*, was finally released in 2007. On this double album, the live versions of 'The Grand Wazoo' and 'Big Swifty' sound close to the original studio versions, at least with regard to the statement of themes. On 'The Grand Wazoo' the original format is followed, with ensemble sections alternating with solos. Ian Underwood contributes competent keyboards, with funky piano fills and a synthesiser solo that provides a contrast to the original by Don Preston. Other solos are by Ray Reed on clarinet, Tony Duran on slide guitar, Bruce Fowler on trombone, substituting for Billy Byers, Sal Marquez on trumpet, and Zappa on guitar. The theme of 'Big Swifty' is stated by the full orchestra, and then a series of solos are played over a medium-fast rock-funk tempo instead of the shuffle tempo used on *Waka/Jawaka*. An alto sax solo by Charles Owens and a trumpet solo by Sal

Marquez prepare the way for Zappa's solo guitar. Interestingly, at 7:08, behind Marquez's solo, the orchestra starts playing a riff from 'Las Vegas Tango', from the album *The Individualism of Gil Evans* (1964), further emphasizing a possible Evans influence on Zappa's music at this time. 'Big Swifty' then draws to a finale, as on the studio recording.

'Approximate' is a piece that Zappa introduced into his repertoire with the touring Grand Wazoo. In the October, 1972, Warner/Reprise circular he described it thus:

> In this selection, the choice of the pitches played by each musician is left up to him (or her). There are only a few bars in the whole piece where a pitch is specified ... The players are requested to adhere to the rhythmic schematic ...
>
> *(Zappa 1972, 3)*

With this piece Zappa was, in effect, following the principles of chance or aleatory music laid down by John Cage and followers like Earle Brown, who created a style of musical construction known as 'Open Form' (see, for instance, Smith Brindle, 1986). As previously noted, Brown organized the 1957 sessions with Edgar Varèse and a group of eminent New York jazz musicians. The jagged, dissonant sound of the theme statement of 'Approximate' places it somewhere between avant garde jazz and new music. After the theme, a series of solos follows over a slow rock-funk tempo. A bass clarinet solo by Mike Altschul is reminiscent of Eric Dolphy, while Ian Underwood's synthesiser solo conjures up the sound of Louis and Bebe Barron's electronic score for the 1956 science-fiction movie *Forbidden Planet*. Other solos are by Earl Dumler on sarrusophone (an instrument related to the bassoon), drums, percussion and Ruth Underwood on marimba.

'The Adventures of Greggery Peccary', which Zappa had written in the early part of 1972, was premiered by the touring Grand Wazoo, and appears on the *Wazoo* album. It is divided into four movements, and lacks the narration that Zappa provided for it on the version on the album *Studio Tan* (1978). From a jazz point of view this recording of 'Greggery Peccary' is interesting because, as Zappa announces in his preamble, 'We're gonna put some solos in between the movements.' In Movement II, a Bolero feel commences at 3:01, and the solo trumpet of Sal Marquez enters at 3:25. A mood not unlike that of 'Solea', from Miles Davis's *Sketches of Spain* (1960), is evoked. As the trumpet solo continues, the bolero rhythm accelerates and at 5:25 becomes a rock tempo. At 6:14 this changes into a tango rhythm behind Tom Malone's tuba solo and then at 7:02 Bruce Fowler's trombone takes over in typically humorous style. In Movement III, between 1:40 and 3:19, Jay Migliori plays a strong, muscular hard-bop tenor saxophone solo, and then, around 5:35, orchestral music that suggests the final, slow build-up in Stravinsky's 'Firebird' (1910) begins to play behind Earl Dumler's humorously lugubrious sarrusophone solo. Zappa's guitar, when it appears at 9:07, creates an ambience that is oblique, reflective and Moorish. This live version of 'Greggery Peccary', then, contains sections of jazz and Third Stream music.

The other two pieces on *Wazoo* are 'Penis Dimension', from *200 Motels* (1971), and 'Variant I Processional March', which later appeared on *Sleep Dirt* (1979) with the title 'Regyptian Strut'. Though each, in its own way, reflects interesting aspects of the orchestral Zappa, neither has any jazz content of special note.

CHAPTER 18

THE PETIT WAZOO

After the final concert with the Grand Wazoo, Zappa decided that he would tour with a smaller version of this ensemble and he retained the services of Malcolm McNab, Bruce Fowler, Glenn Ferris, Tom Malone, Earl Dumler, Tony Duran, Dave Parlato and Jim Gordon. Sal Marquez was replaced by Gary Barone (born 12th December 1941), an excellent jazz trumpeter who had worked with Stan Kenton, Gerald Wilson, Bud Shank, Shelly Manne and Sarah Vaughan. At the end of October 1972 this group embarked on a tour which took in the USA and two dates in Canada, and which finished in San Francisco on 15th December 1972. The group was billed as Frank Zappa and the Mothers of Invention, and it was only later that they were referred to as the Petit Wazoo, for instance in the Zappa interview with Den Simms that appears in *Society Pages* (1990).

Apart from one selection retained from the Grand Wazoo era, namely 'Waka/Jawaka', the Petit Wazoo played a completely new repertoire (Charles Ulrich provides an excellent source of information regarding this group on his *Planet of my Dreams* website at www.members.shaw.ca/fz-pomd.). New versions of pieces played by previous Zappa bands, such as 'America Drinks and Goes Home', 'Chunga's Revenge', 'Duke of Prunes', 'Son of Mr. Green Genes' and 'Willie The Pimp' were included, and new pieces 'Cosmik Debris', 'Don't You Ever Wash That Thing?', 'Farther Oblivion', 'Imaginary Diseases', 'Little Dots', 'Montana', 'Rollo', 'Oddients', 'Been to Kansas in A Minor' and 'Trudgin' Across The Tundra' received their premier performances. Only one complete CD, *Imaginary Diseases* (2006), has been released containing material by this group, and a further single track, 'Trudgin' across the Tundra', is included on the CD *One Shot Deal* (2008). To hear the full repertoire, one must turn to audience recordings, and this is unfortunate because in some ways the Petit Wazoo was even more interesting than the Grand Wazoo, and it would be good to hear the full range of their work, which covered straight-ahead jazz, jazz-rock, blues-rock, avant-garde and contemporary classical music, on legitimate recordings.

The Petit Wazoo horn section contained two trumpets and two trombones which were augmented in a variety of ways, by Tom Malone playing either piccolo trumpet, trombone, tuba, piccolo or tenor saxophone, and by Earl Dumler playing oboe, English horn, sarrusophone, soprano saxophone or baritone saxophone. Thus, a wide palette of tone colours was available. On some pieces, such as 'Imaginary Diseases', where Tom Malone played trombone, a strong, brassy, fanfare-like effect was created. Also, as Charles Ulrich comments on his website, the latter piece is reminiscent of Zappa's Main Title theme from the movie *Run Home Slow*.

Possibly the most interesting piece in the Petit Wazoo's

repertoire was 'Farther Oblivion', a suite lasting 16:02 (on the *Imaginary Diseases* CD) which combines three previously-unheard works, namely the 'Steno Pool' section from 'Greggery Peccary', 'Be-Bop Tango' and 'Cucamonga'. Here, the 'Steno Pool' section is played as an atmospheric big-band jazz waltz, and features some jazzy guitar lines by Zappa. At 2:46 the tempo changes to 4/4 and Tom Malone plays a tuba solo similar to those played by Howard Johnson with the Gil Evans orchestra when Malone was also a member, for instance on the 1974 recording *The Gil Evans Orchestra plays the Music of Jimi Hendrix*. At 4:48 'Be-Bop Tango' commences. This was written by Zappa especially for trumpeter Malcolm McNab, and was initially known simply as 'The Malcolm McNab'. As the latter comments, in the notes to his album *Exquisite* (2006), 'The line was technically awkward and seemed to be heavily influenced by Edgar Varèse ... Needless to say, I still practice the lines of this piece ...' In the same notes, Bruce Fowler says 'I believe that 'Be-Bop Tango' ... is one of Zappa's great masterpieces. I spoke to him about it once, mentioning that it was almost a 12-tone piece'. After the theme statement, the tempo changes at 7:44 to a fast waltz and Bruce Fowler enters with a virtuoso trombone solo that conjures up the spirit of the great Frank Rosolino. Zappa comps jazzily behind the solo. A drum solo by Jim Gordon leads, at 14:31, into 'Cucamonga', played here as another big-band jazz waltz with an intricate theme and brass fanfares. Although Zappa would have found the idea laughable, 'Farther Oblivion' would not have been out of place on a programme of Third Stream music assembled by Stan Kenton or Gunther Schuller.

'Little Dots' can be heard on YouTube in a performance from 29th October, 1972 at Harper College, Binghamton, New York. It is a piece in the same vein as 'Approximate', premiered by the Grand Wazoo. In the theme, pitches appear to be random, while the rhythm is set. The Cagean, chance music approach is used and an avant-garde jazz sound is created. The theme is played by three trumpets plus Earl Dumler on oboe, and a bass/drum duet and a series of solos follow.

'Rollo' and 'Don't You Ever Wash That Thing?' are examples of rhythmically and melodically complex jazz-rock. The former contains a fragment of 'Zomby Woof', later to appear on *Over-Nite Sensation* (1973), and themes that were later incorporated into 'St. Alfonzo's Pancake Breakfast', on *Apostrophe (')* (1974). 'Don't You Ever Wash That Thing?' later appeared on *Roxy and Elsewhere* (1974). 'Trudgin' across the Tundra', released in 2008 on the CD *One Shot Deal*, is a riff in 7/4 which serves as the basis for a fluent, Freddie Hubbard-esque flugelhorn solo by Gary Barone.

As with other large-scale Zappa projects, the musicians involved with the Grand and Petit Wazoos were generally very impressed with Zappa's abilities. In a 2002 interview with Jon Naurin and Charles Ulrich on the latter's *Planet of my Dreams* website, Gary Barone had some interesting comments about his time with the Petit Wazoo:

> This was probably one of the jazziest of Frank's bands. He would come and play at the jam sessions in some of the cities on the tour. He seemed to get off playing with the jazzers. He was amazing. Although he didn't come

from the jazz idiom, he wanted to learn more – and sounded good doing it. I really respected him: his ability to put out so much music and so many ideas … I liked Frank a lot.

(Ulrich 2002)

When Harvey Siders spoke to Grand Wazoo members Jay Migliori, Mike Altschul, Charles Owens, Kenny Shroyer and Glenn Ferris for an article published in *Downbeat* magazine in 1972, their response was "It's a challenge … it's something different … I thought he was crazy at the outset, but there's a method to his madness." Despite his best efforts, Zappa was appreciated by jazz musicians.

CHAPTER 19

THE GEORGE DUKE YEARS

In early 1973 Zappa formed a new band. Significantly, 1973 was the year that post-*Bitches Brew* jazz-rock fusion gained momentum with a string of album releases from major artists and groups, including *Birds of Fire* by The Mahavishnu Orchestra, *Hymn of the Seventh Galaxy* by Return to Forever, *Sweetnighter* by Weather Report, *Headhunters* by Herbie Hancock and *Spectrum* by Billy Cobham. In his own distinctive way, Zappa, with his new band, fitted perfectly into this company, having assembled a group of musicians who were more than adept at playing in the fusion idiom. Foremost in this group was George Duke, who would make a strong individual contribution to Zappa's music for the next two-and-a-half years. In Charles Shaar Murray's 2003 Radio 3 programme, Duke said:

> By '73 I had toured for two years with Cannonball Adderley, and played with Sonny Rollins, Dexter Gordon, Joe Henderson, I'd played with Flora Purim and Airto, Sarah Vaughan, Ella Fitzgerald, you name it, Joe Williams, all these greats of jazz. And so, I was ready for Frank. I said, OK, I'm ready for you, you're getting ready to do a

little more jazz, even though you won't admit it – I feel that he embraced it, but he just didn't tell anybody, he became a fan.

(Shaar Murray 2003, BBC Radio 3)

For his part, Zappa helped Duke to enter the world of jazz fusion more completely by encouraging him to use synthesizers. Duke, in Coryell and Friedman (1978), said:

I was interested, but not really. Finally Frank said, 'Hey, man, you'd be great.' And I said, 'No – there's too many knobs. Just let me play. I'm happy.' So he said okay, but it went on and he prodded me a little … Frank needed a synthesizer in the band, so he bought one and put it in front of me and just left it there … Then, he bought a minimoog and put that in front of me, and eventually I learned how to play them.

(Coryell and Friedman 1978, 152)

Also in the new band were previous Zappa players Sal Marquez, Bruce Fowler, Ian Underwood and Ruth Underwood. Jean-Luc Ponty, after his Zappa-produced solo album and guest appearance on *Hot Rats*, returned to the Zappa fold with an eye to the exposure that would move his international career forward: he would later work with John McLaughlin's Mahavishnu Orchestra and then lead his own successful jazz-rock fusion band. On bass was Bruce Fowler's brother Tom (born 10th June 1951), while the new drummer was Ralph Humphrey (born 11th May 1944), who, after four years with the Don Ellis Orchestra, combined the essence of all the *Hot Rats* drummers – John Guerin, Paul Humphrey and Ron Selico – in his playing. The new band immediately had a distinctive sound which resulted from unusual chord voicings strongly featuring marimba, violin and trombone.

With his new rhythm section of Duke, Fowler and Humphrey, Zappa was also able to convincingly incorporate an element that was becoming an essential aspect of fusion, namely funk. As has been previously mentioned, George Duke had absorbed the jazz-funk influences of Herbie Hancock, and Hancock himself had been strongly influenced by the music of James Brown, Sly and the Family Stone and Stevie Wonder, as Stuart Nicholson (1998) discusses. The funk bass playing of Larry Graham with Sly Stone, and Bootsy Collins with James Brown, was also hugely influential, as was the clavinet sound used on records like 'Outa-Space' by Billy Preston (1971) and 'Superstition' by Stevie Wonder (1972). An example of the way that this Zappa band was able to play funk par excellence occurs in the middle section of 'Dinah-Moe Humm', from *Over-Nite Sensation* (1973). It sounds even better on the extended version on the album *Have I Offended Someone?* (1997), especially from 1:42 – 6:01. *Over-Nite Sensation* also hints at Funkadelic's 1971 album *Maggot Brain*: Zappa's spoken narratives bear a certain resemblance to that of George Clinton, when he talks on the title track about 'tasting the maggots in the mind of the universe', while 'Dirty Love' has a similarly aggressive feel to that of the track 'Super Stupid'. Intriguingly, George Clinton has often used the horn riff from *Over-Nite Sensation's* 'I'm the Slime' in concert (Greenaway, 2014).

That Zappa was now a part of the world of fusion was demonstrated by a tour that he and The Mothers played with The Mahavishnu Orchestra in May, 1973, with Mahavishnu opening the shows. In a discussion that takes place on the DVD *The Drummers of Frank Zappa* (2009), Ruth Underwood comments on the impact that The Mahavishnu Orchestra had on her:

> ... I distinctly remember walking into this gigantic hall, and actually physically feeling being blown back. I'd never had experience of such force, of such volume, and Billy Cobham ... and I took one look at Frank, and I'm telling you, his face changed, and I thought to myself, something major is going to be happening, and sure enough ... new music ... Frank thought, I wanna blow those people out of their chairs too, and suddenly there was a change in the wind, and it was different ... the other thing that was rubbing salt in the wounds was the presence of Jerry Goodman on violin, so you have Jean-Luc and Jerry Goodman, so we could no longer be unique – here's this other machine up on stage, with the same instrumentation.

At this juncture in the discussion, fellow discussant Terry Bozzio remarks,

> Someone told me that this was like a clash of the titans, and both Zappa and McLaughlin would be cranked in their dressing rooms, just gnat-noting out, warming up for their respective shows, and I'm sure Jean-Luc was a little bit frightened, and Jerry as well.

Ruth Underwood continues:

> And also, John McLaughlin was extremely charismatic …
> and there was a real force to that – Frank was no longer
> the only charismatic person in the room, so to speak …
> and I remember looking up from something we were
> playing, 'T'Mershi Duween', and I saw something
> peripherally, and it was Billy Cobham clocking us, and I
> went 'Yeah!' – he was amazed. And I thought, 'OK, it
> works both ways'.
>
> *(The Drummers of Frank Zappa DVD 2009)*

So Zappa was very aware of what was happening in jazz-
rock fusion: he was determined that he would not be
outdone, and that he would make his own unique
contribution in this area of music. And other musicians were
listening and absorbing what he was doing.

The band, with a core membership of George Duke and
Tom Fowler, would last until May, 1975. Ruth Underwood
was part of that core until December 1974, and other band
members came and went: by autumn, 1973, Sal Marquez,
Jean-Luc Ponty and Ian Underwood were gone and
vocalist/flautist/saxophonist Napoleon Murphy Brock
(born 7th June 1945) and drummer Chester Thompson (born
11th December 1948) had joined. Overall, though, this band
maintained its own distinctive character throughout its
existence. A vivid impression of the sound of the first
version of the band playing live can be gained from listening
to the album *Road Tapes Venue # 2* (2013), recorded in
Finland in August 1973: one hears dazzling versions of

instrumentals like 'Big Swifty' and 'Farther O'Blivion', featuring audacious jazz solos from Ponty, Duke, Bruce Fowler and Ralph Humphrey. It is interesting that at this time, as noted by Roman Garcia Albertos (1998), Zappa was using a quote from a Charles Mingus piece, namely 'Trio and Group Dances', from *The Black Saint and the Sinner Lady* (1963). The quote occurs, for instance, at the beginning of 'Dupree's Paradise', on *Roxy by Proxy* (2014), and in 'Be-Bop Tango', on *Roxy and Elsewhere* (1974). George Duke, in Charles Shaar Murray's 2003 Radio 3 programme, said:

> That was a great, great band, because we were stupid, we were efficient in what we did, and there was a lot of jazz in it, I loved it … I have never been in a band that tight … Roxy and Elsewhere happens to be my favourite Frank Zappa record.
>
> *(Shaar Murray 2003, BBC Radio 3)*

Duke's artistry contributed greatly to a number of ferociously difficult and cartoon-esque instrumental pieces that were introduced into the repertoire by Zappa, including 'RDNZL', 'Inca Roads', 'Dupree's Paradise', 'T'Mershi Duween' and 'Spider of Destiny'. Duke plays straight-ahead jazz solos on the original versions of 'RDNZL' and 'Inca Roads' that appear on *The Lost Episodes* (1996) and his virtuoso work is a centre-piece of the version of 'RDNZL' on *Studio Tan* (1978). On 'Regyptian Strut' (*Sleep Dirt*, 1979) he contributes funky licks to the stately theme that had been premiered by the Grand Wazoo Orchestra. On 'Dupree's Paradise', from *Piquantique* (1991), he duets with Zappa on fragments of jazz warhorses 'On Green Dolphin Street' and 'Satin Doll' and then goes into a 'history of jazz piano' routine featuring stride piano, gospel piano, funky organ, funky piano, Red Garland-style block chords and a Cecil Taylor-style freak-out. The *Roxy and Elsewhere* (1974) version of 'Be-Bop Tango' sees him scat singing and quoting from Thelonious Monk's 'Straight No Chaser', and on 'Flambay', from *Sleep Dirt* (1979), his Erroll Garner-inspired playing invokes melodies reminiscent of the standards 'Laura' (David Raksin, 1945) and 'Fly Me To The Moon' (Bart Howard, 1954). In these latter examples he co-conspires (one wonders how willingly) in Zappa's mickey-take of jazz ('Bebop scholars unite' … 'Jazz is not dead, it just smells funny') but the game is given away: the jazz makes a genuine contribution to the music, and Zappa secretly knows all this stuff.

Duke helped to spread the sound of Zappa's type of fusion via his own albums. 'That's What She Said' and 'Giant Child Within Us – Ego', from *I Love The Blues, She Heard My Cry* (1975) reflect Zappa's influence in their complexity, and a version of 'Echidna's Arf', from *Roxy and Elsewhere* (1974), appears on *The Aura Will Prevail* (1975). On the album *The Billy Cobham/George Duke Band Live on Tour in Europe* (1976) the track 'Space Lady' has the science-fiction silliness of 'Earl of Duke', his feature with the 1974 Zappa band (on *A Token of His Extreme Soundtrack*, 2014), while 'Juicy' has hints of 'Inca Roads', especially the version on *One Size Fits All* (1975). Duke also appeared with Cobham on the track 'Life Is Just a Game' on the Stanley Clarke album *School Days* (1976). The Zappa-friendly nature of this track is reflected in its multi-sectioned, rhythmically intricate construction. In a wider sense, the Zappa sound was making noticeable ripples in the fusion pond, and musicians were increasingly taking notice. For instance, Vinnie Colaiuta, who was to become Zappa's drummer in 1978, said, in an interview with Robyn Flans in the November 1982 edition of *Modern Drummer* magazine, that he had always been a big fan of Zappa's and had every record. He thought the music 'was funny and it was musically great'.

CHAPTER 20

BOZZIO, O'HEARN AND ZAPPA IN NEW YORK

In April 1975 drummer Chester Thompson left Zappa to join Weather Report, and was replaced by Terry Bozzio (born 27th December 1950). The latter was a native of San Francisco, and, as told to Robin Tolleson in the November 1981 edition of *Modern Drummer* magazine, he was a thoroughly-schooled musician who had studied at the College of Marin, where, as part of his training, he was called upon to play many classical works. Through his friend, trumpeter Mark Isham, he became familiar with the music of Miles Davis, John Coltrane, Tony Williams and Elvin Jones, and in the early 1970s he was a member of the Latin/rock/jazz-fusion group Azteca, formed by brothers Coke and Pete Escovedo. As he recounted to Robin Tolleson,

> When I was in Azteca I met Eddie Henderson, and I started playing with him and all these other black jazz people around San Francisco. I played with Woody Shaw, and Julian Priester, Joe Henderson, and Luis Gasca, and really had a ball. That was a lot of fun in those days. And

> Eddie used George Duke on one of his albums, and
> George said Frank was looking for a drummer.
>
> *(Tolleson 1981, 23)*

Zappa had hired another musician with a solid jazz background. Bozzio's first recording with his new boss was the album *Bongo Fury* (1975), and he was then able to show the range of his strengths and abilities in the music recorded by Zappa's Abnuceals Emuukha Orchestra in September 1975, which appeared on the album *Orchestral Favorites*, released in 1979. Another track from these sessions, appearing on *QuAUDIOPHILIAc* (2004), was 'Rollo', resurrected from the Petit Wazoo era. This piece of jazz-rock/Third Stream music allowed Bozzio to demonstrate his forceful playing and dynamic fills. A good example of his work in Zappa's next band is his funk playing and drum solo on the version of 'Chunga's Revenge' which appears on the album *Joe's Menage* (2008). This track is also notable for a soulful, David Sanborn-esque alto saxophone solo by Norma Jean Bell.

In the summer of 1976, Patrick O'Hearn (born 6th September 1954) was recruited as Zappa's new bass player. A native of Los Angeles, he had studied cello, violin and flute, and his first gig on bass was as a nine-year-old playing standards in his parents' nightclub act, as described in a *Keyboard* magazine interview with Jeff Burger in January 1987. He became a professional musician aged 15, playing in nightclubs in Portland, Oregon, and after studying with eminent jazz bassist Gary Peacock, he moved in 1973 to San Francisco, where he worked with jazz musicians Charles Lloyd,

Joe Henderson, Dexter Gordon, Joe Pass, Woody Shaw, Eddie Henderson and Bobby Hutcherson. He auditioned for the bass spot in Chick Corea's Return to Forever, before Stanley Clarke got the gig, as reported by Dominic Milano in *Keyboard* magazine in September 1988. In effect, he was moving in the same musical circles as Terry Bozzio, who, in edition 28 of *T'Mershi Duween* magazine, recounted to Andrew Greenaway how O'Hearn joined Zappa:

> Patrick was playing with Joe Henderson at the Lighthouse and I went to see him one night. He was staying at my house. He had this big bass in the car and as he didn't want to leave it in the car, he brought it inside. That was how he auditioned for Frank. He said 'You play that thing?' Patrick said 'Yeah!' He goes 'Whip it out!' and he put him in the studio. Patrick had already played a gig at two or three that morning and he had to play 'The Ocean Is The Ultimate Solution' as sort of an audition. So he got the gig and played great bass through it.
>
> *(Greenaway 1992, 19)*

Bozzio described how the track 'The Ocean Is the Ultimate Solution' came about:

> What actually happened was that Frank, Dave Parlato and I jammed at the Record Plant for about thirty-five minutes and filled up two reels of tape. Zappa, out of all that material, edited it down to about thirteen minutes. He played it on a real interesting Fender twelve-string ... (ibid., 19)

O'Hearn overdubbed double bass on the track, playing a solo between 5:40 and 6:50 in a style not unlike that of Eddie Gomez (as evidenced by his work with Bill Evans, for instance on *At the Montreux Jazz Festival, 1968* or with Chick Corea on 1975's *The Leprechaun*). The track appeared on the album *Sleep Dirt* (1979). He had also been listening to Jaco Pastorius, as is demonstrated by his bass guitar solo on 'Advance Romance', from the album *Philly '76* (2009). In his 1995 biography of Pastorius, Bill Milkowski describes how Jaco, after the release of his solo album and Weather Report's *Black Market* in the summer of 1976, was hailed as the musician who was creating a unique, revolutionary approach to the electric bass.

Along with another San Francisco-based musician, the outstanding soul/gospel-based vocalist Ray White, Zappa's autumn 1976 band was completed by the British ex-Roxy Music keyboardist and violinist Eddie Jobson (born 28th April 1955). Following in the footsteps of Jean-Luc Ponty, Jobson can be heard playing a heartfelt violin solo on 'Black Napkins' from *Philly '76* (2009).

The main focus of Zappa's work in December 1976 was a series of live shows in New York which took place at the Palladium on the 26th, 27th, 28th and 29th December. These formed the basis of the album *Zappa in New York* (1978). Prior to this, the Zappa band made a promotional appearance on the New York-based TV show *Saturday Night Live* on 11th December, playing three numbers in a fifteen-minute spot. For these it was augmented by the *Saturday Night Live* band, a group of some of the best musicians in New York, as well as the returning Ruth Underwood, who would also appear on the Palladium dates. On one of the numbers, 'The Purple Lagoon', the band was joined by the comedy actor John Belushi in his role as the character Samurai Futaba, inspired by Toshiro Mifune's character in Akira Kurosawa's film *Yojimbo* (1961). Belushi had appeared in this role in a number of *Saturday Night Live* sketches, as Bob Woodward (1985) relates, for instance in 'Samurai Delicatessen', where he sliced tomatoes in mid-air with his katana, and 'Samurai Divorce Court', where a custody case was resolved by splitting the children in two. In 'The Purple Lagoon', Belushi played the part of a Samurai bebop saxophonist who interspersed his playing with vocalisations that were a mixture of Samurai war cries and scat singing à la Dizzy Gillespie on, for instance, 'Oop-Pop-A-Da' (1947). This was a situation that no doubt appealed greatly to Zappa: he could put the New York session musicians, another group of 'those goddamned jazz guys with II-V-I' through their paces with the complexity of 'The Purple Lagoon', while Belushi poked fun at bebop. 'The Purple Lagoon', featuring Belushi, can be seen at Vimeo.com.

For the Palladium dates, Zappa again augmented his band with a horn section, plus an extra percussionist. These were all stellar musicians, the cream of the New York jazz, fusion and session scenes. From the *Saturday Night Live* band came trombonist Tom Malone, who had previously worked with Zappa in the live Wazoo bands, multi-reed player Lou Marini (born 13th May 1945), who had played with Zappa musicians Sal Marquez and Bruce Fowler at North Texas State University in 1968, and baritone saxophonist Ronnie Cuber (born 25th December 1941), a veteran of the bands of George Benson, Slide Hampton, Maynard Ferguson and Woody Herman. Vibraphonist Dave Samuels (born 9th October 1948) was noted for his work with, among others, Gerry Mulligan and Carla Bley. The stars of this auxiliary outfit were the Brecker brothers, trumpeter Randy (born 27th November 1945) and tenor saxophonist Michael (29th March 1949 – 13th January 2007). Virtuoso musicians, they had participated in Dreams, the Horace Silver group, the Billy Cobham band and innumerable recording sessions, and their band The Brecker Brothers was one of the premier fusion groups of the time. Cook and Morton (2004) voice a unanimous feeling when they state that Michael Brecker became one of the most admired and emulated saxophonists in contemporary jazz.

The latter was interviewed about his experience with Zappa by the Evil Prince in edition 57 of *T'Mershi Duween* magazine. Brecker stated that

> … we enjoyed working with Frank … He knew exactly what he wanted, and was an extremely hard worker … Frank called me some time after that as he had written a piece for orchestra and saxophone and he wanted me to play the saxophone. I forget why, but I couldn't do it at the time … I think he was also interested in my brother and me. We were coming much more out of swing roots and Frank was coming from weird grouplets of like five and seven and thirteen, so I think when he'd hear someone who would just play simple swing, it affected him … He was a very serious musician; he was not kidding around. He spent an enormous amount of time

studying his craft and coming up with music that was …
Brilliantly put together.

(Evil Prince 1997, 13)

So here was yet another eminent jazz and session musician who admired and respected Zappa. And the respect was obviously mutual: Brecker was a featured soloist on three of the numbers from the New York sessions, namely 'Sofa', 'Black Napkins' (on *You Can't Do That on Stage Anymore Vol. 6*, 1992) and 'Approximate/The Purple Lagoon'. His work, technically brilliant yet always soulful, was, as ever, immediately recognizable. It is interesting to speculate what the Zappa/Brecker orchestral collaboration might have sounded like: undoubtedly it would have been very different from the one Brecker recorded with Claus Ogerman in 1982 on the album *Cityscape*.

The album *Zappa in New York* is notable for many reasons: one is that it heralded the debut of 'The Black Page', a composition that has become a rite of passage for any jazz fusion drummer worth his or her salt. As stated by Greg Rule in the April 1991 edition of *Drums & Drumming* magazine:

It's 30 bars of sight-reading hell: a twisted, polyrhythmic joyride of 32nd-notes and bizarre triplet groupings. The mere mention of its ominous name is enough to send shivers rocketing up and down the spine, and for good reason.

(Rule 1991, 55)

Terry Bozzio, in a July 1994 *Modern Drummer* magazine

interview with Rick Mattingly, explained the origin of 'The Black Page', describing how he had incorporated a Tony Williams lick into his solos during his time with Zappa:

> It was like a Swiss triplet with a foot beat in it, broken up around the toms. It had a quintuplet type of feel in terms of being five notes. I had pretty much ripped it off note-for-note from a Stanley Clarke album that Tony Williams played on. Frank thought that it was interesting enough that he used it in the introduction to 'The Black Page'.
>
> *(Mattingly 1994, 23)*

The Tony Williams solo occurs at the beginning of the track 'Power', on Stanley Clarke's eponymous 1974 album, and it is interesting to compare it to Bozzio's solo at the end of the track 'Manx Needs Women', which leads directly into 'The Black Page Drum Solo/Black Page # 1'. Williams, one of the all-time great jazz drummers, had indirectly inspired a Zappa composition.

In the previously-cited *Modern Drummer* interview from November 1981, Bozzio described how, as a direct result of the *In New York* sessions, he came to join the Brecker Brothers band the following year:

> When Zappa's band played with the Brecker Brothers, it was automatic hook up, you know. We just really dug each other, and had loads of fun playing in the solos and stuff. And they sat behind me, and watched me burn through all these shows in New York. They said, 'Look, we're going to be doing some stuff, and we'd like you to come

and play with us.' So when we had a break with Zappa –
he wasn't doing anything all through the summer – I was
contacted by them, and I said I'd do it … coming from
jazz and fusion music, that was my chance to really get
my rocks off …So with Neil Jason and Barry Finnerty
[Bozzio's guitarist friend from San Francisco] we just
burned every night for a whole month.

(Tolleson 1981, 24)

The results, heard on the live album *Heavy Metal Bebop*,
recorded in 1977, but released in 1978, demonstrate a further
link between Zappa and jazz fusion.

The instrumental music on *Zappa in New York*, in the way
that Zappa arranges for the brass and reeds, is in many ways
a logical extension of the music from the Grand and Petit
Wazoo eras. 'Approximate', from that period, with a stunning
exposition of the theme, is combined with 'The Purple
Lagoon', and the latter's 7/4 pulse provides a basis for
extended solos by Michael Brecker, Ronnie Cuber recalling
Pepper Adams on Charles Mingus's *Blues & Roots* (1959),
Patrick O'Hearn, again acknowledging the work of Jaco
Pastorius and also inserting a quote from Thelonious Monk's
'Blue Monk', and Randy Brecker using a harmonizer that
duplicates his trumpet sound in other pitches. The result is
state-of-the-art mid-1970s fusion with the unique Zappa
extra ingredient.

Other instrumentals include powerful versions of 'A
Pound for a Brown' and 'Cruisin' for Burgers', to which the
brass and reeds contribute with effortless force. 'Manx
Needs Women' is a startling, jagged piece of atonal music,

while 'I Promise Not To Come In Your Mouth' is, unusually for Zappa, quietly romantic, nodding in the direction of classic tunes like, for instance, 'Invitation' by Bronislau Kaper (1952). In 6/4 and the key of C minor, with subtle chord changes, it provides a platform for a thoughtful guitar solo by Zappa, who proves again that he can solo in a fluent jazz style. There is also a rhapsodic synthesiser solo by Eddie Jobson. One has the impression that Zappa, embarrassed at having written such a genuinely moving piece of music (he referred to it sarcastically in the album sleeve notes as 'a sensitive instrumental ballad for late-nite easy listening'), immediately attempted to cancel out the effect by giving it a crude title. Fortunately, he did not succeed, and, interestingly, the piece was retitled 'Läther' on the album of the same name (1996).

'The Black Page Drum Solo', featuring the combined efforts of Terry Bozzio and Ruth Underwood (plus later studio overdubs), acknowledges the influence of Varèse's 'Ionisation', while the staggering, lurching rhythms and strange, imperious melody lines of 'The Black Page #1 and #2' push forward the boundaries of fusion and Third Stream music. 'Punky's Whips' moves through a series of movements, alternating Terry Bozzio's vocals with typically complex passages and a nightmarish version of the 1932 Rodgers and Hart song 'Isn't It Romantic', allowing Zappa to take another pot-shot at the Great American Songbook. 'The Torture Never Stops' features some jazzy little touches, with a haunting flute riff and, as on *Uncle Meat*, some Ray Crawford-like chording by Zappa.

Zappa in New York is a milestone album in Zappa's

oeuvre. It develops the orchestral timbres of *Lumpy Gravy* and *The Grand Wazoo*, and constructs a bridge between New York jazz fusion and Zappa's own unique vision. And in gaining the respect of New York's finest, Zappa could yet again put 'those goddamn jazz guys' in their place, while tacitly allowing jazz to influence his music.

CHAPTER 21

WOLF, MARS AND MANN

In the summer of 1977 Zappa formed a new band. While retaining the services of Patrick O'Hearn and Terry Bozzio, he brought in three new members who each had a strong jazz background. These were keyboard players Peter Wolf and Tommy Mars, and percussionist Ed Mann. Peter Wolf (born 26th August 1952) was a native of Vienna, Austria and studied classical piano at Vienna's Conservatory of Music, as he discussed with Mr. Bonzai in an interview in the November 2007 edition of *Keyboard* magazine. At the age of sixteen, having developed an interest in jazz through his father's influence, he won the solo pianist category in the European Jazz Festival. He played with a number of European jazz and fusion bands and moved to the United States in 1975, working first in Atlanta and Birmingham before moving to Los Angeles. As he said in the liner notes to *Hammersmith Odeon* (2010), 'I was a hardcore jazzer. Miles, Trane, Parker and Weather Report were my heroes.' He was introduced to Zappa by ex-Zappa keyboard player Andre Lewis. Ed Mann (born 14th January 1954) discussed his background with Rick Mattingly in the August 1982 edition of *Modern Drummer*. He studied at Hartt College of Music,

Connecticut and then, in 1973, moved to California to study with highly-regarded percussionist John Bergamo at the California Institute of the Arts. The latter had been involved in recording orchestral pieces with Zappa, and in 1977 he and Mann worked on the overdubs for 'The Black Page', which had been recorded for the *Zappa in New York* album in 1976. This led to Mann joining Zappa and recommending Tommy Mars, who he had known since 1971. Tommy Mars (born 26th October 1951) also studied at Hartt College of Music, and worked as a solo pianist, choirmaster and organist. As stated in an interview with Evil Prince in the October 1997, edition 61 of *T'Mershi Duween* magazine, he was influenced by pianists Art Tatum, Chick Corea, Keith Jarrett and McCoy Tyner. He moved to California, and at the time he joined Zappa, he was working at the Biltmore Hotel in Santa Barbara.

The new band, apart from all its other capabilities, was able to play state-of-the-art jazz fusion, as is demonstrated on the album *Hammersmith Odeon* (2010), recorded in early 1978. The track 'Pound for a Brown' features a vibraphone solo in 7/8 by Ed Mann which prefigures the work of Mike Mainieri with his classic fusion band Steps, later Steps Ahead (not formed until 1979, as reported on Mainieri's NYC website). Mann is followed by a keyboard solo by Peter Wolf which is divided into three parts. In the first section, the 7/8 tempo continues as Wolf plays a probing solo on Electrocomp synthesiser, leading into an out-of-tempo section on Yamaha electric grand. This develops into a 4/4 shuffle featuring Minimoog, reminiscent of Jan Hammer's work on, for instance, the album *Jeff Beck with the Jan Hammer*

Group Live (1977). Everything is underpinned by the unstoppable drive of Terry Bozzio's drums as he showcases his unique variation on Billy Cobham's style. Bozzio, one of the most influential drummers to emerge in the 1970s, is able to give full rein to his abilities on his solo feature 'Terry Firma'. Tommy Mars's inimitably eerie scat singing, in unison with his keyboard playing, makes a strong impression on 'Little House I Used to Live In' and a driving version of 'King Kong'.

CHAPTER 22

BARROW AND COLAIUTA

In the summer of 1978 there were further changes to the band when bassist Arthur Barrow and drummer Vinnie Colaiuta joined. Again, each had a comprehensive musical background that included jazz. Arthur Barrow (born 28th February 1952) had been a Zappa fan since his teens, as he states on his web site, and studied at North Texas State University from 1971 to 1975, graduating with a Bachelor of Music degree with a major in composition specializing in electronic music. During his time at North Texas he absorbed the music of, among others, Stockhausen, Bartok and John Coltrane. In 1975 he moved to Los Angeles with one of his main goals being to play with Zappa. He recorded with The Doors on their album *American Prayer* (1976) and worked in a jazz fusion band called Loose Connection with Zappa alumni Bruce Fowler and Don Preston before his Zappa audition in June 1978. Vinnie Colaiuta (born 5th February 1956) started playing drums as a child and some of his early influences were Tony Williams, Miles Davis, John Coltrane and Elvin Jones. After studying at Berklee College between 1974 and 1975 he played with the Fowler Brothers band, which led to his audition with Zappa. Colaiuta quickly showed himself to be an outstanding, virtuoso player with a special, natural ability to play polyrhythms, and was soon being ranked among the best jazz fusion drummers. For instance, in the November 1981 *Modern Drummer* interview, Terry Bozzio, who Colaiuta had replaced, said 'Vinnie Colaiuta … is now my favourite drummer.' This was praise indeed.

The brilliance of the new rhythm section was demonstrated on a piece entitled 'Mo's Vacation', recorded live in September 1978, and appearing on Disc One of *Beat the Boots III* (2009). Played by Ed Mann on marimba, Barrow and Colaiuta, 'Mo's Vacation' set a new standard of virtuosity to which both jazz fusion and classical musicians could aspire. Terry Bozzio, in the previously mentioned interview, said:

> It's really off the wall. It's ridiculously hard, some parts are very fast, and it's melodically very difficult. It's like Zappa said, 'This is to make The Black Page obsolete.'
>
> *(Tolleson 1981, 24)*

And Colaiuta's solo ability, audacious but relaxed, is shown on the track 'Zeets', recorded in October 1978 and appearing on the album *Halloween* (2003).

There are other tracks from the autumn 1978 period that demonstrate the jazz capabilities of this Zappa band. A version of 'A Pound for a Brown', from the album *Saarbrucken 1978* (1991), is similar to, but even better than, the one recorded earlier in the year at Hammersmith Odeon. Again, there is the prefiguring of Steps Ahead with Ed

Mann's 7/8 vibraphone solo, but this gives way to a fast, straight-ahead-swing keyboard solo in 4/4 on Rhodes by Peter Wolf, sounding like Herbie Hancock and driven by Vinnie Colaiuta's intensely swinging drums. Wolf continues to swing as he switches to Electrocomp synthesiser, suggesting the brass section of a big band, and winds things up with an out-of-tempo Minimoog extemporization. Other examples of the solo virtuosity of both Wolf and Tommy Mars on a version of 'A Pound for a Brown' appear on *You Can't Do That On Stage Anymore Volume 4* (1991).

Patrick O'Hearn had left the band but returned for some dates in autumn 1978 to form a two-bass line-up with Arthur Barrow. He can be heard on the track 'Lobster Girl' on *You Can't Do That Onstage Anymore Volume 6* (1992), again showcasing his Jaco-esque skills in a scintillating duet with Vinnie Colaiuta. The same album features violinist L. Shankar as a guest, following in the footsteps of previous Zappa violinists Sugarcane Harris, Jean-Luc Ponty and Eddie Jobson. Shankar, as described in a November 2, 1978 *Downbeat* feature by Lee Underwood, was born on 26th April 1950, and had worked with Archie Shepp before forming the group Shakti with John McLaughlin. He met Zappa when he was playing with McLaughlin's One Truth Band and German dates were shared in August and September 1978. Shankar plays a lilting solo on 'Thirteen', which alternates between 5/8 and 4/4, and can also be heard on a jaunty, fusion-lite but musically precise version of 'Take Your Clothes Off When You Dance', which also features solos by vibraphone and keyboards.

A number of tracks by the 1978/1979 band, specifically

showcasing Zappa's solo guitar work, feature on the *Shut Up 'N Play Yer Guitar* series of albums (1981). As Kasper Sloots (2012) discusses, Zappa had a preference for using the three modal scales, namely the Dorian, Lydian and Mixolydian. This was because, as he said in a November 1991 *Musician* interview with Matt Resnicoff, 'I pretty much *loathe* chord progressions'. Reference has previously been made, in the section on *The Grand Wazoo*, to Brett Clement's (2009) comment on the connection between Zappa's music and modal jazz, and this is relevant to his solo style. As Clement says:

> In modal jazz ... the improviser is allowed greater melodic freedom through the use of scalar modes in conjunction with slowly shifting or static harmonies ... Though Zappa never admitted to any influence of modal jazz, it is possible that some of the innovations of modal jazz were absorbed into his music ... harmonic stasis and improvisatory melody are trademarks of his style.
>
> *(Clement 2009, 104)*

Certainly, a track like the haunting 'While You Were Out' captures the ambience of modal jazz. Another aspect of the tracks on the *Shut Up* albums is what Kasper Sloots refers to as the 'wildly irregular rhythmic groupings'. Ted Gioia (2009), in an article entitled 'The Jazzy Side of Frank Zappa', discusses the track 'Five-Five-FIVE', noting how 'Zappa flies over an intricate pattern which juxtaposes 5/8 and 5/4 ... I am just as impressed by the rhythm section and especially Vinnie Colaiuta's drumming'. Colaiuta talks about this in the November 1982 *Modern Drummer* interview:

He said, 'I want you to listen to what I'm playing because I'm playing all these rhythms. When you accompany me, I don't want you to just try to guess what they are and play some standard rhythmic fill. I want you to understand exactly where I'm at and communicate with me on that level.' That forced me to try to improvise these polyrhythms and think in that way, which is not the norm by any stretch of the imagination. People just don't do that.

(Flans 1982, 46)

Rhythmic complexity was also a feature of the album *Joe's Garage*, recorded in mid-1979. Colaiuta, in the same interview, discusses the track 'Keep It Greasey' and observes

There's this one part where the actual time signature is 19/16. The feel is like it is 4/4 with three 16th notes tacked onto the end of it. Then there's another part in 21. It was all one live take; no splices or adds or anything. We just rehearsed it.

(Flans 1982, 48)

So an influential musician like Colaiuta was able to take the information that he learned while with Zappa and, in his post-Zappa career, project it into the wider musical world, including that of jazz.

During the autumn tour of 1980, Zappa began to use a vocal style, as Neil Slaven (1996) relates, known as *Sprechstimme* (speaking voice) or *Sprechgesang* (speech song). It was a technique previously used by composers like

Schoenberg, for instance in his 1912 composition 'Pierrot Lunaire'. Ben Watson (1994) accurately describes it as 'Zappa's leering silly-voice taunting' and, in a February 1987 interview in *Music Technology* magazine with Rick Davies, Zappa described how he incorporated this voice into a process called Meltdown:

> ... depending on what's in the news that day, or what happened in the audience during the show, I'd start talking in a singsong tone of voice and then Tommy Mars would chop changes behind it. Now that's very freeform, kind of like 'The Dangerous Kitchen' or 'The Jazz Discharge Party Hats'; those are both meltdown events. In the case of 'The Dangerous Kitchen', it's a fixed set of lyrics that has variable pitches and variable rhythms. In the case of 'The Jazz Discharge Party Hats', it was completely spontaneous, 100% improvised by me and the band.
>
> *(Davies 1987, 50)*

Thus, 'The Dangerous Kitchen' and 'The Jazz Discharge Party Hats' (both on *The Man from Utopia*, 1983) use improvised jazz backings, the latter with a very fast swing tempo. Another interesting example occurs in a version of 'The Torture Never Stops', from the album *Buffalo* (2007). At 2:48 there is a quote from 'Chattanooga Choo Choo', the 1941 standard by Harry Warren and Mack Gordon: Zappa takes another pot-shot at The Great American Songbook, and then he recites the 'Torture' lyrics over an almost Cecil Taylor-like backing by Tommy Mars. At 10:47, after Zappa's guitar solo, there is a long, exciting jazz solo in 3/4 by Mars, on Rhodes, Electrocomp and Minimoog, followed at 14:32 by a relaxed, swinging and technically jaw-dropping drum solo by Vinnie Colaiuta. A further example of *Sprechstimme* and jazz piano on the *Buffalo* album occurs on 'Buffalo Drowning Witch'. Jazz had a subliminal but strong presence in the music of the autumn 1980 band: another instance of this appears on 'The Madison Panty-Sniffing Festival' on *You Can't Do That Onstage Anymore Volume 6* (1992), where the band plays a cool version of the Benny Golson jazz standard 'Killer Joe' behind Zappa's narration.

Guitarist Steve Vai (born 6th June 1960) joined the band for the autumn 1980 tour. Having attended Berklee College of Music aged eighteen, he had initially worked for Zappa as a music transcriber. For the final versions of 'The Dangerous Kitchen' and 'The Jazz Discharge Party Hats' which appeared on *The Man from Utopia* album, Vai transcribed Zappa's vocal lines, then overdubbed an acoustic guitar part on the live recordings.

CHAPTER 23

MARTIN, THUNES AND WACKERMAN

By the summer of 1981, with the departure of Colaiuta and Barrow (although the latter stayed on as rehearsal supervisor), three new musicians had been recruited to the Zappa rhythm section, namely Robert (Bobby) Martin, Scott Thunes and Chad Wackerman. These three would remain as the core of the band until its demise after the final tour in 1988. Robert Martin (born 29th June 1948), as he described to Evil Prince in the July 1996, edition 52 of *T'Mershi Duween* magazine, grew up in Philadelphia, the son of two opera singers, and, because of the eclectic attitude of his parents and the strong musical atmosphere of his home city, he was exposed to many types of music, including big band swing and jazz. He studied French horn at the Curtis Institute, and, after hearing David 'Fathead' Newman with the Ray Charles band, was inspired to teach himself tenor saxophone. He also became an accomplished pianist and vocalist. After working with Etta James and the band Orleans, he brought his many skills to the Zappa band. Scott Thunes (born 20th January 1960) began playing bass aged ten and, like Terry Bozzio, studied music at the College of Marin, as he told Thomas Wictor in the latter's book *In Cold Sweat* (2001).

119

While at college he was in a band playing jazz, jazz-rock and 'all sorts of stuff that didn't really relate directly to my musical studies'. Chad Wackerman (born 25th March 1960) came from a musical family, started playing drums at six, and at eleven began attending Stan Kenton Jazz Clinics, as he told Dave Levine in the May 1983 edition of *Modern Drummer* magazine. After attending Cal State University he played with the Bill Watrous big band and quartet, and recorded three albums with Watrous in 1980.

Some of Zappa's most brilliant instrumental pieces gained prominence as part of the repertoire of the 1981/1982 band. These included 'Drowning Witch', 'Envelopes' (both on *Ship Arriving Too Late to Save a Drowning Witch*, 1982), 'Moggio' (on *The Man from Utopia*, 1983), 'Sinister Footwear II', 'Marqueson's Chicken' (both on *Them or Us*, 1984), 'Alien Orifice' and 'What's New In Baltimore' (both on *Frank Zappa meets The Mothers of Prevention*, 1985). All were notable for the unique sonorities created by the blends of synthesiser, percussion and guitar, and passages of stunning complexity, for instance the section in 'Alien Orifice' between 2:33 and 3:14. Typical of these instrumentals is 'What's New in Baltimore', with an opening section containing a sequence of short melodies in keys and meters that keep changing. 'Marqueson's Chicken' is in 13/16 and 'Moggio' is in 10/8. In contrast, the laconic, loping swing of the theme of 'Alien Orifice' brings to mind jazz pieces like the previously-mentioned 'Killer Joe' by Benny Golson, or Lalo Schifrin's version of George Gershwin's 'Prelude # 2' on his album *New Fantasy* (1964) (this is not as far-fetched as it may sound: in the July 2004 edition of *Mojo* magazine

Schifrin stated that Zappa 'was a friend and a genius'). All these pieces, in pushing forward standards of musicianship and composition, though not typical of the jazz fusion repertoire, would undoubtedly provide inspiration for musicians working in that, and other, fields.

A piece that does fit more comfortably into the jazz fusion arena is 'Clowns on Velvet', recorded live at The Ritz in New York in November 1981 and appearing on Disc One of *Beat the Boots III* (2009). Yet again, Zappa seemed to be attempting to show that he could write music, in whatever genre, better than anyone else. Indeed, with its fast samba-funk feel, 'Clowns on Velvet' would have fitted well into a Chick Corea set, and ex-Corea guest guitarist Al Di Meola plays a barnstorming solo, while Chad Wackerman hits a Steve Gadd-type groove. The basic track, with overdubs, appeared again on *Thing-Fish* (1984). Also on *Thing-Fish*, jazz musician Jay Anderson played double bass on the tracks 'The Massive Improve'lence' and 'Briefcase Boogie'. Anderson (born 24th October 1955) had worked with the Woody Herman orchestra and Carmen McRae, and was recommended to Zappa by his old friend Chad Wackerman. Anderson's walking bass, accompanied by Wackerman's jazz drums, can be heard on 'The Massive Improve'lence' behind Ike Willis's narration. He also overdubbed double bass on the tracks 'The Dangerous Kitchen' and 'The Jazz Discharge Party Hats' for the CD remix of *The Man from Utopia*. In a comment on the *United Mutations* website Anderson (1999) said 'I was the only person at the session ... He [Zappa] was very respectful, wanted my input, and was great to work with'. Here was yet another jazz/session musician who was impressed with Zappa as a person and as a musician.

In contrast to the regularly positive reaction that session musicians registered after working with Zappa, he included a song on *Frank Zappa meets The Mothers of Prevention* (1985) entitled 'Yo Cats' which portrayed them as mercenary union men who were prepared to play sterile music for high financial returns. Yet again he displayed his paradoxical attitude.

In the summer of 1984 keyboard player Allan Zavod replaced Tommy Mars. Zavod, an Australian, was influenced in his playing by Herbie Hancock, Keith Jarrett, McCoy Tyner and Bill Evans, as he told Dominic Milano in the April 1978 edition of *Contemporary Keyboard* magazine, and he had an impressive track record. Educated at Melbourne Conservatorium of Music between 1965 and 1969, he then studied at Berklee College, Boston. In the early 1970s he worked with the Glenn Miller orchestra, Mike Gibbs and Gary Burton, the Maynard Ferguson orchestra, the Thad Jones/Mel Lewis orchestra and jazz-rock group New York Mary. After working with Billy Cobham, he moved on to the band of Jean-Luc Ponty. Zavod had a solo feature with the 1984 Zappa band on 'Let's Move to Cleveland', and one example of this appears on *Does Humor Belong in Music* (1986). In an intense, driving, bravura performance where he shows all his jazz influences, he builds up to a climax that particularly reflects the work of McCoy Tyner. Another example of this solo feature, equally exciting, appears on *You Can't Do That On Stage Anymore Volume 4* (1991). The latter performance, recorded at Amherst, Massachusetts, is also interesting because it features a guest appearance by tenor saxophonist Archie Shepp, who at this time was a lecturer at the University of Massachusetts, Amherst (Carr, 1987). Renewing his acquaintance with Zappa from New York in 1967 and Amougies in 1969, Shepp can be heard delivering a solo that, typically for him, mixes the influence of Coleman Hawkins with emotionally vocalized sounds. In 1984, Zappa was still quietly allowing jazz to contribute to his music.

In 1986 Zappa released an album entitled *Jazz from Hell*, which, apart from one track, contained music created on his Synclavier Digital Music System. Questioned by Rick Davies in the February 1987 edition of *Music Technology* magazine about the album's title, Zappa said, 'You know the expression: if there's somebody in show-business and he's an asshole, he can be referred to as an Entertainer from Hell. It arrived from that type of concept. This is it. If this is Jazz, then it's Jazz from Hell'. The title track would certainly be regarded as hellish by the sort of mainstream jazz fan who dislikes musicians like Ornette Coleman and Cecil Taylor: with a slight imaginative leap it conjures up what Taylor might sound like playing 'Le Marteau sans Maître' by Pierre Boulez. The album's first track, 'Night School', has a lofty, imperious sound, a haunting quality and an intricately weaving melody line. It seems like a logical successor to 'Peaches en Regalia', both in its attractiveness and its potential appeal to jazz musicians, and a big band version has been recorded by Ed Palermo on his album *Eddy Loves Frank* (2009) while orchestral versions have been recorded by Joel Thome on the *Zappa's Universe* album (1993) and by Ensemble Modern on *Greggery Peccary & Other Persuasions* (2003). 'G-Spot Tornado' is an amusing and exciting piece that has lent itself to both orchestral and jazz interpretations: the former on *The Yellow Shark* (1993) and the latter in a big band arrangement by Ed Palermo on the Tommy Igoe album *New Ground* (1996). Palermo's arrangement stays true to the spirit of the original while opening up its jazz potential with a Stan Kenton-ish latin feel.

CHAPTER 24

THE LAST BAND

In the summer of 1987, not having toured since 1984, Zappa decided to form another band and commenced rehearsals. The core of the band consisted of previous Zappa alumni, namely Ike Willis, Robert Martin, Ed Mann, Scott Thunes and Chad Wackerman. This band would tour America and Europe between February and June 1988, and would be his last. Interestingly, like the 1976 New York band, it was a large ensemble of eleven pieces and had a five-piece horn section featuring trumpet, trombone, alto, tenor and baritone saxophones. The ambience of the New York band was continued and extended: sensational versions of old and new Zappa pieces, as well as cover versions of other composers' works, were created, while incorporating a more sustained jazz feel than had been heard in any of Zappa's previous bands, with scope for extended solo work by the horn players. Typically and paradoxically, in the midst of all this jazz influence, Zappa could not resist mocking jazz musicians and fans, as is evidenced by the album *Make a Jazz Noise Here* (1991).

The use of a five-piece horn section followed directly in the jazz tradition of medium-sized groups which, via the use of clever arrangements, could produce a big sound while avoiding the economic problems resulting from using a full big band, usually with fifteen or sixteen members. In the modern jazz era, the Miles Davis *Birth of the Cool* band (1949-1950) was a major influence in this respect, using trumpet, trombone, French horn, tuba, alto saxophone and baritone saxophone. On the West Coast this approach was used by leaders like Shorty Rogers and Lennie Niehaus, and on the East Coast by musicians like Charles Mingus and George Russell. Dizzy Gillespie used the exact trumpet/trombone/alto/tenor/baritone line-up on his album *The Greatest Trumpet of Them All* (1957), as did Quincy Jones on certain tracks on *This Is How I Feel about Jazz* (1957). In a 1996 interview with Evil Prince in issue 56 of *T'Mershi Duween* magazine, trombonist Bruce Fowler commented that '… in 1988 he [Zappa] went all the way and had five [horns], which is the best. Five is really big-sounding and you can do those big chords he writes'. Significantly, Fowler also said 'I was interested to find that Frank was interested in jazz. Even in the earliest days (sings the opening theme to 'Take Your Clothes off When You Dance'). I never realised how much of a jazz tune it was'.

Bruce Fowler returned to the Zappa fold in 1988 after an absence of thirteen years. In the first part of his *T'Mershi Duween* interview in issue 55 he provided a lengthy list of the jazz trombonists who had influenced him. These included J.J. Johnson, Carl Fontana, Urbie Green, Curtis Fuller, Albert Mangelsdorff, Jack Teagarden and Frank Rosolino. This is a veritable cornucopia of great jazz trombonists, but one who is missing, and who also appears to have been a strong

influence on Fowler, is Bill Harris. The latter is best known
for his work with the Woody Herman orchestra in the 1940s.
Harris had a zany sense of humour and this was often
reflected in his playing, which featured slurring effects and
sudden brassy outbursts. Typical examples of these effects
occur on 'Wildroot' and 'Blowin' up a Storm', recorded by
Herman in 1945. On recordings from the 1988 Zappa tour
Bruce Fowler can frequently be heard demonstrating his Bill
Harris-type humour. For instance, on 'Big Swifty', from *Make
a Jazz Noise Here* (1991), his solo changes from straight-ahead
improvisation into Bill Harris mannerisms and a quote from
the 1932 Cole Porter standard 'Night And Day'. Again, on
'Dupree's Paradise', his virtuoso solo moves through tempo
changes before reflecting a humorous Harris influence.

The 1988 brass section was completed by Bruce's
brother Walt (born 2nd March 1955) on trumpet and
flugelhorn. A lyrical, fluent, Freddie Hubbard-inspired player
who was perhaps the outstanding jazz soloist in the band,
Walt Fowler assumed the role taken by Randy Brecker in
1976. He had previously played briefly with Zappa in 1974,
and then pursued a busy career with Billy Cobham, the
Fowler Brothers Band, Michael White, the LA Jazz Quintet,
Luis Conte and Brandon Fields.

As Scott Thunes describes in Andrew Greenaway's book
Zappa the Hard Way (2010) the three 1988 reed players were
all friends of the Fowler brothers. On alto and soprano
saxophone was Paul Carman (born 31st December 1955),
receiving his first major musical exposure. Tenor saxophonist
Albert Wing (born 19th July 1952) began clarinet when he
was aged nine, and at thirteen he moved on to tenor and

baritone sax. As he said to Fred Banta (2000) in issue 63 of
T'Mershi Duween magazine, he listened to Charlie Parker, John
Coltrane and 'a lot of the artists from the bebop days'. At
Westminster College, Salt Lake City, he came under the
influence of Dr. William Fowler and began his association
with the Fowler brothers, appearing on a number of their
albums. As a soloist Wing is very much influenced by
Michael Brecker, and it is interesting to compare his solos
on 'Black Napkins', on *Make a Jazz Noise Here* (1991), and
'Sofa', on *The Best Band You Never Heard in Your Life* (1991),
with those of Brecker in the 1976 New York band.

Kurt McGettrick (1ˢᵗ July 1946 – 6ᵗʰ May 2007) played
baritone and bass saxophones and contrabass clarinet. A
graduate of Berklee College of Music, he appeared on Cal
Tjader's album *Huracon* (1978) with fellow jazz musicians
Clare Fischer and Frank Rosolino, and recorded the albums
Hot (1979) and *Perspectives* (1982) with the Steve Spiegl big
band. He also worked with Tom Petty, Patti LaBelle and
Phoebe Snow. McGettrick appears to be an unsung hero of
the reed instruments, and it is interesting to read the tributes
paid to him on the *Sax on the Web* website. He is referred to
as being 'like an American John Surman' and on tenor
saxophone it is felt that his favourite influence was Gene
Ammons. Steve Marsh (2007) says that 'His advanced
techniques on bari sax, bass sax, bass clarinet, contrabass
clarinet, flute, alto flute and piccolo were astounding', and
discusses his solo on 'King Kong' on *Make a Jazz Noise Here*
(1991), saying that it 'displays many of his stylistic traits.
Melodic and thematic development, upward leaps of several
octaves, very fast doubling tonguing, huge reverberating

multiphonics, insanely high altissimo, real fast runs that are precisely articulated. And always swinging'.

Mike Keneally (born 20th December 1961) completed the band's line-up. He provides a definitive source of information at www.Keneally.com. A San Diego resident only previously known for leading his band Drop Control, he was a virtuoso musician who played guitar and keyboards, and was also a vocalist and composer. He had an encyclopaedic knowledge of Zappa's repertoire, having studied it from the age of ten, and stepped into the role of stunt guitarist previously filled by Steve Vai.

Despite conflicts within the band that eventually led to its premature breakup, it was, in the opinion of many, the best that Zappa ever had. Certainly, it was tight, exciting and virtuosic, and produced stunning versions of Zappa favourites like 'Florentine Pogen', 'Andy', 'Inca Roads' and 'Zomby Woof', all of which appear on *The Best Band You Never Heard in Your Life* (1991). As an account of the band and its demise, Andrew Greenaway's 2010 book is invaluable.

The mainly instrumental album *Make a Jazz Noise Here* (1991) does just that, despite Zappa's extended poke at jazz on 'Big Swifty'. On this track, after the statement of the theme, Zappa, with heavy irony, issues the command 'Make a jazz noise here!' and a laughing Ike Willis makes exclamations throughout the rest of the track like 'Go, man, wild!' and 'Wild man, yeah!' After Bruce Fowler's solo there is a manic Spike Jones-inspired instrumental passage quoting Wagner's 'Lohengrin', Bizet's 'Carmen' and Tchaikovsky's '1812 Overture' and then the listener is launched into Robert Martin's cool, walking jazz piano accompanied by a synthesised voice making 'Aye … aye … aye' noises. In his April 1990 *Society Pages* interview with Den Simms, Zappa says 'You ever heard of Erroll Garner, who mumbles along with what he plays? … It's the whole concept of jazz musicians who make jazz noises while they perform'. From 6:10 to 6:56 the horn section riffs, utilizing distinctly Ellingtonian sonorities, and then the tempo doubles and Albert Wing dives into an exciting, Brecker-ish solo. The mickey-take of jazz musicians and fans who take themselves too seriously *is* funny, but one feels that Zappa labours the point and has to spoil good jazz with silly voices and Spike Jones-isms. He still can't let those II-V-I guys off the hook. In the above-mentioned *Society Pages* interview he also indicates that the members of his horn section became very precious when working out their parts for 'The Untouchables Theme' (on *Broadway the Hard Way*, 1988), and he mockingly suggests that they were thinking 'Jeezus Christ! I'm a jazz musician! Should I really be doing this?'

A powerful version of 'Dupree's Paradise', possibly the definitive one, provides a platform for a vibrant flugelhorn solo by Walt Fowler, and Bruce Fowler moves through tempo changes with both virtuosity and humour. The backing for Albert Wing's fast swing-tempo solo is reminiscent of parts of 'How Did That Get in Here?' on *The Lumpy Money Project/Object* (2009), and Paul Carman's alto is featured in an impassioned, bluesy freakout. Both 'Black Napkins' and 'Sinister Footwear' take on new, jazzier musical personalities as a result of the succession of horn solos that they feature. 'The Black Page' and 'Alien Orifice' also reveal new facets, the former in its languid, insinuating, 'New Age' version and the latter sounding, in its opening section, like a cross between Blue Note hard bop and the Brecker Brothers.

On *The Best Band You Never Heard in Your Life* (1991) Zappa resurrects 'The Eric Dolphy Memorial Barbecue' after an absence from the repertoire of fifteen years. Again, this is the most seriously jazzy recorded version of this piece, with another fine flugelhorn solo by Walt Fowler. Other solos include Paul Carman on alto saxophone, paying his own tribute to Eric Dolphy, and Ed Mann with a fast, swinging vibraphone solo.

Eric Dolphy's colleague Oliver Nelson also received a tribute from the 1988 band. Zappa had always liked Nelson's tune 'Stolen Moments', as he acknowledged in 1989 on the NPR radio show *John McNally's Castaway Choice* when he included it in ten favourite records (this is noted, for instance, by Marc De Bruyn (2003) on the globalia.net website). 'Stolen Moments' appears on the album *Broadway the Hard Way* (1988), capturing the authentic haunting, melancholy Nelson sound with a version that falls somewhere between the original recording of the tune that appeared on Eddie 'Lockjaw' Davis's album *Trane Whistle* (1961) and Nelson's own version on his album *Blues and the Abstract Truth* (1961), featuring Dolphy, Freddie Hubbard and Bill Evans. Walt Fowler plays yet another excellent solo, capturing the spirit of Hubbard's original. 'Stolen Moments' was played between February and March 1988 in the USA and between April and June 1988 in Europe, as Andrew Greenaway (2010) records. Audience recordings reveal that it was a vehicle for extended solos by, at different times, Bruce Fowler, Paul Carman, Kurt McGettrick, Ed Mann and Robert Martin, scat singing along with his piano solo. And on a number of occasions, Zappa himself played very creditable jazz solos. Here he was, actually improvising over the chord sequence of a jazz standard, despite 'pretty much loathing chord sequences'. It seems that, with his final band, Zappa was able to acknowledge more fully than ever before the contribution that jazz made to his music.

CHAPTER 25

POSTSCRIPT

Frank Zappa died on the 4th December, 1993. During his professional career, he had been keenly aware of everything that had happened, and continued to happen, in 20th century American culture. Sponge-like, he soaked in all the cultural influences around him, stored them, and ultimately regurgitated them in an original synthesis, as the author has attempted to show elsewhere (Wills, 2013). Jazz was one such cultural influence, and it made a significant contribution to his work. The purpose of this book has been to clarify what that contribution was.

Zappa was a complex person, and a vulnerable one, due to early life events. He tried to disguise his vulnerability from anyone who might take advantage of it, and had a talent for hiding in plain sight. He gave the impression of being a straight talker, while omitting or altering pertinent facts, as he did in his story of the incident with Duke Ellington in *The Real Frank Zappa Book*. He was frequently disparaging about jazz, but meanwhile he had provided, if one looked in the right places, a long list of jazz musicians whose work he admired, including Roland Kirk, Charles Mingus, Eric Dolphy, Cecil Taylor, Bill Evans, Wes Montgomery, Sun Ra,

Miles Davis, Oscar Pettiford, Thelonious Monk, Harold Land, Archie Shepp and Oliver Nelson. Zappa was a jazz fan but he just didn't like to admit it. The majority of his band members, from Don Preston in the 1960s to Albert Wing in 1988, were talented jazz players.

Zappa shared similarities with certain jazz leaders. Miles Davis, in successive groups, gave prominence to several outstanding musicians such as John Coltrane, Cannonball Adderley, Bill Evans, Wayne Shorter, Herbie Hancock and Tony Williams. In the same way Zappa gave Jean-Luc Ponty, George Duke, Terry Bozzio, Vinnie Colaiuta, Steve Vai and Chad Wackerman their first major exposure. Duke Ellington formed his own publishing company and composed, performed and recorded non-stop, leaving a huge discography. Zappa followed his example, and, as Peter Lavezolli (2001) has pointed out, like Ellington, he broke down the barriers between popular and serious art forms. In Ellington's band, specific musicians were showcased in certain pieces of music, for instance Harry Carney in 'Sophisticated Lady' and Johnny Hodges in 'Jeep's Blues'. In the same way, Zappa's musicians had their own showcases, including George Duke in 'RDNZL' and Terry Bozzio in 'The Black Page'.

Many musicians who worked with Zappa had also worked with eminent jazz orchestras. For instance, George Duke, Ralph Humphrey, Dave Parlato, Glenn Ferris and Mike Altschul had all worked with Don Ellis, and Kenny Shroyer, Mike Altschul, Earl Dumler, John Rotella, Ray Reed, Gary Barone, Jay Migliori, Shelly Manne, Frank Capp, Max Bennett, Vince DeRosa, Richard Perissi, Arthur Maebe, Emil

Richards and Dennis Budimir had all worked at different times with Stan Kenton. Odd as it may seem, there were certain similarities between Zappa and Kenton. Although Kenton was very different to Zappa in certain ways, being accused of being both reactionary and humourless (Easton, 1973), both were California-based workaholics, and both recorded a huge body of work that was extremely diverse in musical scope while always retaining an identifiably individual sound. Both used popular works to finance their more serious classical projects: in Zappa's case, 'Dinah-Moe Humm' helped to pay for working with the London Symphony Orchestra, while Kenton's popular records with vocalists like June Christy paved the way for his forty-piece Innovations in Modern Music orchestra. Kenton's recording of Bob Graettinger's 'City Of Glass' (1951), which Gunther Schuller (1995) said sounded like Charles Ives, might well have appealed to Zappa. Both Kenton and Zappa loved loud, dissonant brass chords: the one at 5:53 on 'Improvisation' on Kenton's *New Concepts of Artistry in Rhythm* (1953) is virtually interchangeable with the one at 2:05 on 'I'm Stealing the Towels' on Zappa's *200 Motels*. It would have been interesting to hear Kenton conducting the Los Angeles Neophonic Orchestra (their 1965 album featured a number of musicians who worked with Zappa) in performances of material from *Lumpy Gravy* or *The Grand Wazoo*: both Kenton and Zappa, in their own ways, created forms of Third Stream music.

Reference has previously been made to Zappa's statements that he loathed chord progressions (*Musician*, November 1991) and particularly the II-V-I chord progression (*Musician*, August 1979). Arthur Barrow (2014) has stated that Zappa probably had a particular aversion to pieces like 'Giant Steps' by John Coltrane (1960). Nevertheless, in the same 1979 interview, Zappa said '… there are of course progressions that I like a lot, and I use them all the time. I go for what I like …' He played some excellent solos over (admittedly easier) chord sequences, for instance on the jazzy 'Blessed Relief' (*The Grand Wazoo*, 1972), 'Fifty-Fifty' (*Over-Nite Sensation*, 1973) and 'Alien Orifice' (*Frank Zappa meets the Mothers of Prevention*, 1985).

If Zappa has had any influence on jazz, it is probably mainly in the area of jazz fusion, in a general way and not just via albums like *Hot Rats* and *The Grand Wazoo*. The exceptional standard of musicianship which became the norm in his bands is now the standard to which jazz-based musicians automatically aspire. For instance, in the field of drumming Vinnie Colaiuta, Terry Bozzio and Chad Wackerman have become role models: Colaiuta has won a total of 18 'Drummer of the Year' awards from *Modern Drummer* magazine's annual reader polls, as described in his profile at Drummerworld.com. and Bozzio and Wackerman have performed together in a series of highly-acclaimed drum clinics, as reported by David Aldridge in the June/July 2002 issue of *DRUM!* magazine. Zappa's compositional influence can be seen in Third Stream works by Zappa alumni: *The Universe Will Provide* by Mike Keneally (2004), *Chamber Works* by Terry Bozzio (2005) and *Sound Theories Volume II* by Steve Vai (2007), all recorded with the Metropole Orkest.

In a broader sense, Zappa pieces occur regularly in the

Montgomery, Wes (1960) *The Incredible Jazz Guitar of Wes Montgomery*. Riverside RLP 12-320.

Nelson, Oliver (1961) *Blues and the Abstract Truth*. Impulse AS-5.

Ogerman, Claus (1982) *Cityscape*. Warner Bros 1-23698.

Palermo, Ed (1997) *Ed Palermo Plays the Music of Frank Zappa*. Astor Place TCD-4005.

Palermo, Ed (2006) *Take Your Clothes Off When You Dance*. Cuneiform Rune 225.

Palermo, Ed (2009) *Eddy Loves Frank*. Cuneiform Rune 285.

Palermo, Ed (2014) *Oh No! Not Jazz!!* Cuneiform Rune 380/381.

Ponty, Jean-Luc (1969) *Electric Connection*. World Pacific ST 20156.

Ponty, Jean-Luc (1969) *The Jean-Luc Ponty Experience*. World Pacific ST 20168.

Ponty, Jean-Luc (1970) *King Kong*. World Pacific ST 20172.

Ponty, Jean-Luc (1981) *Live at Donte's*. Blue Note LT 1102.

Preston, Billy (1971) 'Outa-Space'. A & M 1320.

Return to Forever (1973) *Hymn of the 7th Galaxy*. Polydor 2310283.

Richards, Johnny (1955) *Annotations of the Muses*. Légende LP 1401.

Rogers, Shorty (1955) *The Swinging Mr. Rogers*. Atlantic LP 1212.

Rollins, Sonny (1956) *Sonny Rollins Plus 4*. Prestige PRLP 7038.

Schifrin, Lalo (1964) *New Fantasy*. Verve V6-8601.

Scott, Tom (1974) *Tom Scott and the LA Express*. Ode 77021.

Scott, Tom (1975) *Tom Cat*. Ode 77029.

Silver, Horace (1956) *Six Pieces of Silver*. Blue Note BLP 1539.

Sun Ra (1965) *The Heliocentric Worlds of Sun Ra Vol. 1*. ESP 1014.

Thomas, René (1954) *The René Thomas Quintet*. Vogue (F) 7432-162291-2.

Timmons, Bobby (1960) *This Here is Bobby Timmons*. Riverside RLP 1164.

Tiomkin, Dimitri (1960) *The Alamo (Soundtrack)*. Columbia CL 1558.

Towns, Colin and NDR Big Band (2005) *Frank Zappa's Hot Licks (And Funny Smells)*. Rent a Dog 2007-2.

Vai, Steve (2007) *Sound Theories, Vols. I and II*. Epic 88697 01421 2.

Various (1957) *Jazz in Transition*. Transition T3LP 30.

Various (1993) *Zappa's Universe*. Verve 314 513 575-2

Wattles, Bud (1959) *Themes from the Hip*. Roulette R-25073.

Weather Report (1973) *Sweetnighter*. Columbia KC 32210.

Wonder, Stevie (1972) 'Superstition'. Tamla T54226F.

Zappa, Frank (1966) *Freak Out*. Verve MGM V/V6-5005-2.

Zappa, Frank (1967) *Absolutely Free*. Verve V/V6-5013.

Zappa, Frank (1968) *We're Only in it For the Money*. Verve V/V6-5045.

Zappa, Frank (1968) *Lumpy Gravy*. Verve V/V6-8741.

Zappa, Frank (1969) *Uncle Meat*. Bizarre/Reprise 2MS 2024.

Zappa, Frank (1969) *Hot Rats*. Bizarre/Reprise RS 6356.

Zappa, Frank (1970) *Burnt Weeny Sandwich*. Bizarre/Reprise RS 6370.

Zappa, Frank (1970) *Weasels Ripped My Flesh*. Bizarre/Reprise MS 2028.

Zappa, Frank (1970) *Chunga's Revenge*. Bizarre/Reprise MS 2030.

Zappa, Frank (1971) *Frank Zappa's 200 Motels*. Bizarre/United Artists UAS 9956.

Zappa, Frank (1972) *Just Another Band From LA*. Bizarre/Reprise MS 2075.

Zappa, Frank (1972) *Waka/Jawaka*. Bizarre/Reprise MS 2094.

Zappa, Frank (1972) *The Grand Wazoo*. Bizarre/Reprise MS 2093.

Zappa, Frank (1973) *Over-Nite Sensation*. DiscReet MS 2149.

Zappa, Frank (1974) *Apostrophe(')*. DiscReet DS 2175.

Zappa, Frank (1974) *Roxy and Elsewhere*. DiscReet DS 2202.

Zappa, Frank (1975) *One Size Fits All*. DiscReet DS 2216.

Zappa, Frank (1975) *Bongo Fury*. DiscReet DS 2234.

Zappa, Frank (1978) *Zappa in New York*. DiscReet 2D 2290.

Zappa, Frank (1978) *Studio Tan*. DiscReet DSK 2291.

Zappa, Frank (1979) *Sleep Dirt*. DiscReet DSK 2292.

Zappa, Frank (1979) *Orchestral Favorites*. DiscReet DSK 2294.

Zappa, Frank (1981) *Shut Up 'N Play Yer Guitar*. Barking Pumpkin BPR 1111.

Zappa, Frank (1981) *Shut Up 'N Play Yer Guitar Some More.* Barking Pumpkin BPR 1112.

Zappa, Frank (1981) *Return of the Son of Shut Up 'N Play Yer Guitar.* Barking Pumpkin BPR 1113.

Zappa, Frank (1982) *Ship Arriving Too Late to Save a Drowning Witch.* Barking Pumpkin FW 38066.

Zappa, Frank (1983) *The Man From Utopia.* Barking Pumpkin FW 38403.

Zappa, Frank (1984) *Them or Us.* Barking Pumpkin SVBO-74200.

Zappa, Frank (1984) *Thing-Fish.* Barking Pumpkin SKCO-74201.

Zappa, Frank (1985) *Frank Zappa Meets The Mothers of Prevention.* Barking Pumpkin ST-74203.

Zappa, Frank (1986) *Does Humor Belong in Music?* EMI CDP 7 46188 2.

Zappa, Frank (1986) *Jazz from Hell.* Barking Pumpkin ST-74205.

Zappa, Frank (1987) *London Symphony Orchestra Vol. II.* Barking Pumpkin SJ-74207.

Zappa, Frank (1991) *Saarbrucken 1978.* Essential ESMCD 962.

Zappa, Frank (1991) *Piquantique.* Essential ESMCD 963.

Zappa, Frank (1991) *The Best Band You Never Heard in Your Life.* Barking Pumpkin D2 74233.

Zappa, Frank (1991) *Make a Jazz Noise Here.* Barking Pumpkin D2 74234.

Zappa, Frank (1991) *You Can't Do That on Stage Anymore Vol. 4.* Rykodisc RCD 10087/88.

Zappa, Frank (1992) *You Can't Do That on Stage Anymore Vol. 5.* Rykodisc RCD 10089/90.

Zappa, Frank (1992) *You Can't Do That on Stage Anymore Vol. 6.* Rykodisc RCD 10091/92.

Zappa, Frank (1993) *The Yellow Shark.* Barking Pumpkin R2 71600.

Zappa, Frank (1996) *The Lost Episodes.* Rykodisc RCD 40573.

Zappa, Frank (1996) *Lather.* Rykodisc RCD 10574/76.

Zappa, Frank (1997) *Have I Offended Someone?* Rykodisc RCD 10577.

Zappa, Frank (2003) *Halloween*. Vaulternative/DTS 1101.

Zappa, Frank (2004) *QuAUDIOPHILIAc*. Barking Pumpkin/DTS 1125.

Zappa, Frank (2004) *Joe's Domage*. Vaulternative VR 20042.

Zappa, Frank (2006) *Imaginary Diseases*. Zappa Records ZR 20001.

Zappa, Frank (2006) *The MOFO Project/Object*. Zappa Records ZR 20004.

Zappa, Frank (2007) *Buffalo*. Vaulternative VR 2007-1.

Zappa, Frank (2007) *Wazoo*. Vaulternative VR 2007-2.

Zappa, Frank (2008) *One Shot Deal*. Zappa Records ZR 20007.

Zappa, Frank (2008) *Joe's Menage*. Vaulternative Records VR 20081.

Zappa, Frank (2009) *The Lumpy Money Project/Object*. Zappa Records ZR 20008.

Zappa, Frank (2009) *Philly '76*. Vaulternative Records VR 20091.

Zappa, Frank (2009) *Beat the Boots III, Disc One*. Download.

Zappa, Frank (2009) *Beat the Boots III, Disc Three*. Download.

Zappa, Frank (2010) *Hammersmith Odeon*. Vaulternative Records VR 20101.

Zappa, Frank (2013) *Road Tapes, Venue # 2*. Vaulternative Records VR 2013-1.

Zappa, Frank (2013) *A Token of his Extreme Soundtrack*. Zappa Records ZR 20015.

Zappa, Frank (2014) *Roxy by Proxy*. Zappa Records ZR 20017.

Zappatistas (2000) *Live in Leeds*. Jazzprint JPVP 122.

ACKNOWLEDGEMENTS

Throughout the text, where other authors are quoted, the author's name and the page number of the edition used are given. Publication details can be found in the References section.

For comments, suggestions, emails and other help, I am greatly indebted to the following: Arthur Barrow, Jonathan W. Bernard, Paul Buff, Paul Carr, Brett G. Clement, Alex Dmochowski, Chuck Foster, Chuck Glave, Andrew Greenaway, Nigey Lennon, Ed Palermo, Charles Ulrich.

Grateful acknowledgement is made to the following for permission to use extracts:

Excerpt from *Jazz-Rock Fusion: The People: The Music* by Julie Coryell and Laura Friedman, 1978. Used with permission of Marion Boyars Publishers.

Excerpts from 'Frank Zappa: The Mothers of Invention' by Frank Kofsky in *Giants of Rock Music* edited by Pauline Rivelli and Robert Levin, 1981, 1985. Used with permission of Perseus Books Group.

Excerpt from Clifford Allen interview with Buell Neidlinger, 16 December 2003. Used with permission of *www.allaboutjazz.com*

Excerpts from 'Zappa and Jazz' by Ed Palermo, 27 December 2007. Used with permission of *www.allaboutjazz.com*

ACKNOWLEDGEMENTS

The following websites have been exceptional sources of information:

www.globalia.net/donlope/fz/
www.members.shaw.ca/fz-pomd/

INDEX

INDEX

INDEX

repertoires of jazz musicians. Examples include 'Zoot Allures', on tenor saxophonist Javon Jackson's album *A Look Within* (1996), 'Oh No', on the album *Surf's Up* (2001) by pianist David Kikoski and 'Marqueson's Chicken', on pianist Ran Blake's 2005 album *Indian Winter*. 'King Kong' has become something of a jazz standard: a recent version occurs on keyboardist Jeff Lorber's album *Hacienda* (2013). Italian pianist Stefano Bollani included 'Let's Move to Cleveland' on his 2004 album *Smat Smat* and in 2011 he played three concerts of Zappa's music, with the title 'Sheik yer Zappa', in Italy with a band that included American musicians Josh Roseman, Jason Adasiewicz, Larry Grenadier and Jim Black. An album of this music was released in2014.

A number of European jazz orchestras have devoted whole albums to Zappa's music with excellent results, remaining true to the spirit of the music while highlighting the jazz possibilities. The Riccardo Fassi Tankio Band's tribute (1994) has previously been referred to, and also notable are albums by the Swedish Bohuslan Big Band (2000), the French Le Bocal (2003), and the German NDR Big Band, conducted and arranged by Colin Towns (2005). Meanwhile, The Zappatistas, an eight-piece British group led by jazz guitarist John Etheridge, recorded a live album in 1999.

The jazz musician who has shown most dedication to Zappa's music is Ed Palermo. Alto saxophonist, arranger, composer and big band leader Palermo has recorded four albums of Zappa's music: *Ed Palermo Plays the Music of Frank Zappa* (1997), *Take Your Clothes off When You Dance* (2006), *Eddy Loves Frank* (2009) and *Oh No! Not Jazz!!* (2014).

Describing himself as 'an alto saxophonist from the Bird/Cannonball/Phil Woods school' in his 2007 *All About Jazz* article, and as 'someone who has never stopped embracing [his] roots' in the October, 2009 edition of *Downbeat* magazine, he also says that he loves Duke Ellington, listens to him all the time, and incorporates what he has learned from him in his arrangements. However, he also feels that *his* music is the music of the 1960s, and, having listened to Zappa since he was a teenager, he believes that 'Zappa's music is incredible. There's so much to work with. There's a lot of room for jazz musicians … to solo' (*Downbeat*, October 2009, 42). He thinks that 'What Edgar Varèse was to Frank Zappa, Frank Zappa is to me' (*All About Jazz*, 2007, 1). An example of Palermo 'embracing his roots' occurs between 5:53 and 7:01 on his version of 'Echidna's Arf' on *Eddy Loves Frank*, where the saxophone section plays a transcription of Cannonball Adderley's solo on 'Work Song', from his 1960 album *Them Dirty Blues*.

So, in a way, things have come full circle. Throughout his career, Zappa incorporated elements of jazz into his music. With the passage of time, jazz has become broader-based and more able to absorb new influences. The music of Frank Zappa is now, however imperceptibly, feeding back into jazz.

Duke, George (1975) *The Aura Will Prevail*. MPS 5D 064D-99394.

Ellis, Don (1971) *Tears of Joy*. Columbia G 30927.

Ensemble Modern (2003) *Greggery Peccary and Other Persuasions*. RCA Red Seal 82876 56061 2.

Evans, Bill (1968) *At the Montreux Jazz Festival 1968*. Verve V6 8762.

Evans, Gil (1961) *Out of the Cool*. Impulse AS-4.

Evans, Gil (1964) *The Individualism of Gil Evans*. Verve V6-8555.

Evans, Gil (1971) *Blues in Orbit*. Enja 3069.

Evans, Gil (1974) *The Gil Evans Orchestra Plays the Music of Jimi Hendrix*. RCA CPL1- 0667.

Fassi, Riccardo (1994) *Riccardo Fassi Tankio Band Plays the Music of Frank Zappa*. Splasc(H) Records CD H 428.2.

Foster, Chuck (1985) *Long Overdue!* Sea Breeze SB-2023.

Funkadelic (1971) *Maggot Brain*. Westbound WB 2007.

Gillespie, Dizzy (1959) *The Greatest Trumpet of Them All*. Verve MG V-8352.

Gillespie, Dizzy (1995) *The Complete RCA Victor Recordings*. RCA Bluebird 07863 66528 2.

Hancock, Herbie (1969) *Fat Albert Rotunda*. Warner Bros Seven Arts 1834.

Hancock, Herbie (1973) *Headhunters*. Columbia KC 32731.

Herman, Woody (1974) *Thundering Herd*. Fantasy F9452.

Herman, Woody (1997) *Blowin' Up a Storm*. Charly CDGR 162-2.

Hodeir, Andre (1954) *Le Jazz Groupe de Paris*. Swing (F) M33353.

Hubbard, Freddie (1970) *Red Clay*. CTI LP 6001.

Igoe, Tommy (1996) *New Ground*. Deep Rhythm Music DRMTRI-1001.

Jackson, Javon (1996) *A Look Within*. Blue Note CDP7243 8 36490 2 0.

Jaspar, Bobby (1954) *Bobby Jaspar's New Jazz*. Swing (F) M33338.

Jaspar, Bobby (1954) *Bobby Jaspar Sextet*. Vogue (F) ELP 7100.

Jazz Crusaders, The (1962) *The Jazz Crusaders at The Lighthouse*. Pacific Jazz ST-57.

Jones, Quincy (1957) *This is How I Feel about Jazz.* ABC
Paramount ABC-149.

Keneally, Mike (2004) *The Universe will Provide.* Favored Nations
FN 2400-2.

Kenton, Stan (1951) *City of Glass.* Capitol H-353.

Kenton, Stan (1953) *New Concepts of Artistry in Rhythm.* Capitol T-
383.

Kenton, Stan (1965) *Stan Kenton Conducts The Los Angeles
Neophonic Orchestra.* Capitol MAS-2424.

Kikoski, David (2001) *Surf's Up.* Criss Cross Jazz CRISS 1208.

Kross, Mark (1990) *Cacciatore.* T-Bone Music TBCD-4887.

Le Bocal (2003) *Oh No!... Just Another Frank Zappa Memorial
Barbecue!* Le Chant du Monde 274 1258.

Levine, Hank (1961) 'Image'. ABC-Paramount 10256.

Lewis, John (1961) *John Lewis Presents Contemporary Music: Jazz
Abstractions: Compositions by Gunther Schuller and Jim Hall.*
Atlantic 1365.

Lorber, Jeff (2013) *Hacienda.* Heads Up International HUI
34476-02.

Love, Preston (1968) *Preston Love's Omaha Bar-B-Q.* Kent KST-
540.

McFarland, Gary (1969) *America the Beautiful.* Skye SK-8.

Mahavishnu Orchestra (1973) *Birds of Fire.* Columbia KC 31996.

Mainieri, Mike (1994) *White Elephant Vol. 1.* NYC 6008-2.

Mainieri, Mike (1995) *An American Diary.* NYC 6015-2.

Manne, Shelly (1960) *Shelly Manne and his Men at the Black Hawk
Vol. 1.* Contemporary 57577.

McNab, Malcolm (2006) *Exquisite.* Kinnell House Records KHR
1001.

Mingus, Charles (1959) *Blues and Roots.* Atlantic SD 1305.

Mingus, Charles (1959) *Mingus Ah Um.* Columbia CS 8171.

Mingus, Charles (1963) *The Black Saint and the Sinner Lady.*
Impulse AS-35.

Montgomery Brothers, The (1961) *The Montgomery Brothers in
Canada.* Fantasy 3323.

REFERENCES

Adams, John (2002) in conversation with Leonard Slatkin, BBC
    Radio 3, 18 January.
Albertos, Román Garcia (1998) 'The Hook', *Information is not
    Knowledge*, 28 June.
    http://globalia.net/donlope/FZ/songs/The_Hook.html.
Aldridge, David (2002) 'Terry Bozzio and Chad Wackerman:
    Two Zappa Drum Set Vets Team Up for Solo Drumming
    Tour', *DRUM! Magazine*, June/July.
    *http://www.drummagazine.com/features/post/terry-bozzio-chad-
    wackerman.*
Allen, Clifford (2003) 'Buell Neidlinger: From Taylor to Zappa
    to The Carpenters', *All AboutJazz*, 16 December.
    *http://allaboutjazz.com-from-taylor-to-zappa-to-the-carpenters-buell-
    neidlinger-by-clifford-allen.php*
Anderson, Jay (1999) 'Jay Anderson', *United Mutations*.
    http://www.united-mutations.com/a/jay_anderson.htm
Banta, Fred (2000) 'Chatting with A. Wing and a Prayer',
    T'Mershi Duween, 63, March: 20-24.
Barrow, Arthur (2014) in communication with the author.
Barrow, Arthur, website.
    http://home.netcom.com/~bigear/Zappa.html.
Basie, William and Murray, Albert (1986) *Good Morning Blues: The
    Autobiography of Count Basie.* London: Heinemann.
Bava, Mario (1960) *The Mask of Satan (US title Black Sunday).*
    American international Pictures.
Belushi, John (1976) 'Bebop Samurai', *Saturday Night Live*, NBC
    TV, 11 December. http://vimeo.com/45273681

Bock, Richard (1970) quoted by Leonard Feather in sleeve notes
to *Jean-Luc Ponty / King Kong*. World Pacific ST 20172.

Bonzai, Mr. (2007) 'Getting the Call, Giving it All: Peter Wolf
Interview', *Keyboard*, November: 38, 40.

Bourne, Michael (2009) 'Ed Palermo Big Band: Obsessed with
Zappa', *Downbeat*, October: 42-44.

Brindle, Reginald Smith (1986) *Musical Composition*. Oxford:
Oxford University Press.

Buff, Paul (2008) in communication with the author.

Burger, Jeff (1987) 'Patrick O'Hearn and his Digital Laundry',
Keyboard, January: 18.

Cage, John (1960) 'Water Walk', performed on *I've Got a Secret*,
CBS TV, 26 February.
http://www.youtube.com/watch?v=B9vvrSyAPuW

Carr, Ian, Fairweather, Digby and Priestley, Brian (1987) *Jazz: The
Essential Companion*. London: Grafton Books.

Chambers, Jack (2008) *Bouncin' with Bartok: The Incomplete Works of
Richard Twardzik*. Toronto: Mercury Press.

Clement, Brett G. (2009) 'A Study of the Instrumental Music of
Frank Zappa', PhD Thesis, University of Cincinnati,
College-Conservatory of Music.
*http://etd.ohiolink.edu/view.cgi/Clement%20Brett%20G.pdf?acc_
num=ucin 124870891*

Colaiuta, Vinnie (2012) 'Vinnie Colaiuta', *Drummerworld.com*.
http://www.drummerworld.com/drummers/Vinnie_Colaiuta.html.

Colli, Beppe (2012) 'Review: Jean-Luc Ponty/King Kong', *Clouds
and Clocks*.
www.cloudsandclocks.net/CD_reviews/ponty_kingkong_Ehtn

Collier, James Lincoln (1987) *Duke Ellington*. London: Michael
Joseph.

Cook, Richard (1984) 'Frankly, Frank, is Anyone Listening?', *New
Musical Express*, 17 November, p. 15.

Cook, Richard and Morton, Brian (2004) *The Penguin Guide to Jazz
on CD (Seventh Edition)*. London: Penguin.

Coryell, Julie and Friedman, Laura (1978) *Jazz-Rock Fusion: The*

People and the Music. London: Marion Boyars.

Crow, Bill (1993) *From Birdland to Broadway: Scenes from a Jazz Life*. New York: Oxford University Press.

Davies, Rick (1987) 'Father of Invention', *Music Technology*, February: 42, 45, 44-50.

De Bruyn, Marc (2003) 'Stolen Moments', *Information Is Not Knowledge*, 6 September. *http://globalia.net/donlope/FZ/Songs?Stolen_Moments.html*

Delbrouck, Christophe (2008) 'Le Grand et le Petit Wazoo', *Jazz Magazine (France)*, June: 36-38.

Dmochowski, Alex (1993) in communication with the author.

Duffie, Bruce (1988) 'Composer David Raksin: A Conversation with Bruce Duffie'. http://www.kcstudio.com/raksin2.html

Easton, Carol (1973) *Straight Ahead: The Story of Stan Kenton*. New York: Morrow.

Evil Prince (1996) 'Robert Martin Sez Hello', *T'Mershi Duween*, 52, July: 14-18.

Evil Prince (1996) 'The Trombone's connected to the Lip Bone: Bruce Fowler Interview Part I', *T'Mershi Duween*, 55, November: 9-11.

Evil Prince (1997) 'The Trombone's connected to the Lip Bone: Bruce Fowler Interview Part II', *T'Mershi Duween*, 56, February: 24-26.

Evil Prince (1997) 'Getting Randy with Michael Brecker', *T'Mershi Duween*, 57, March: 13.

Evil Prince (1997) 'Mars needs Evil Princes: A Conversation with Tommy Mars', *T'Mershi Duween*, 61, October: 12-19.

Fass, Dave and Street, Dave (1978) 'Phi Zappa Crappa Interview: Peeking into the Mind of Rock and Roll's Original Madman', *Acid Rock*, January.

Flans, Robyn (1982) 'Vinnie Colaiuta', *Modern Drummer*, November: 8-11, 46, 48, 50, 52, 54, 56-58.

Forte, Dan (1979) 'Zappa', *Musician*, August: 34-43.

Foster, Chuck (2008) in communication with the author.

Fricke, David (1979) 'Bad Taste is Timeless: Cruising Down

Memory Lane with Frank Zappa', *Trouser Press*, April: 20-23, 58.

Gilbert, Mark (1997) 'Jean-Luc Ponty', *Jazz Journal*, July: 6-8, 47.

Gioia, Ted (1992) *West Coast Jazz*. New York: Oxford University Press.

Gioia, Ted (2008) 'The Dozens: The Jazzy Side of Frank Zappa', *jazz.com*. http://www.jazz.com/dozens/the-dozens-the-jazzy-side-of-frank-zappa.

Gitler, Ira (1982) Sleeve Notes, *Allen Eager: Renaissance*. Uptown UP 27.09.

Glave, Chuck (2008) in communication with the author.

Greenaway, Andrew (1992) 'One More Time for the World', *T'Mershi Duween*, 28, November: 12-16.

Greenaway, Andrew (2010) *Zappa the Hard Way*. Bedford, England: Wymer.

Greenaway, Andrew (2014) in communication with the author.

Heineman, Alan (1969) 'Boston Globe Festival', *Downbeat*, 1 May, pp. 36-37.

Heineman, Alan (1972) 'The Many Sides of Buell Neidlinger', *Downbeat 17th Annual Yearbook*: 13-15, 36.

Hodenfield, Chris (1970) 'Frank Zappa', *Strange Days*, 11-25 September, pp. 18-19.

Hoskyns, Barney (1996) *Waiting for the Sun: The Story of the Los Angeles Music Scene*. London: Penguin.

James, Billy (2001) *Necessity Is ... The Early Years of Frank Zappa and the Mothers of Invention*. London: SAF Publishing.

James, Billy (2002) in communication with the author.

Kaye, Carol (1998) 'Jazz Musicality Prevails at Pop Recording Sessions', *Downbeat*, March: 70.

Keneally, Mike 'About Mike', *Keneally Dot Com*. *http://www.keneally.com/about-mike/*

Kloet, Co de (1992) 'Happy Together', *Society Pages*, 11, February: 15-22.

Kofsky, Frank (1967) 'Frank Zappa: The Mothers of Invention, Part I', *Jazz and Pop*, September: 1-5.

Kofsky, Frank (1967) 'Frank Zappa: The Mothers of Invention, Part II', *Jazz and Pop*, October: 28-32.

Kubernik, Harvey (2009) *Canyon of Dreams: The Magic and the Music of Laurel Canyon*. New York: Sterling.

Lavezzoli, Peter (2001) *The King of All, Sir Duke: Ellington and the Artistic Revolution*. New York: Continuum.

Leigh, Nigel (1993) 'Frank Zappa', *Late Show Special Broadcast*, BBC2 TV, 17 December.
http://www.youtube.com/watch?=HV1aBxhewE

Lennon, Nigey (1995) in conversation with Bob Dobbs (as communicated to the author by Bob Dobbs, 2011).

Lennon, Nigey (2003) *Being Frank: My Time with Frank Zappa (2nd edition)*. Los Angeles: California Classics.

Levine, Dave (1983) 'Chad Wackerman: Enjoying all Challenges', *Modern Drummer*, May: 15-17, 52, 54, 56.

Lindsell, Alec (2008) *Frank Zappa and the Mothers of Invention in the 1960s*. New Malden: Chrome Dreams Media.

Loder, Kurt (1990) *Bat Chain Puller: Rock and Roll in the Age of Celebrity*. New York: St. Martin's Press.

Lord, Tom (2004) *The Jazz Discography*. CD-ROM, Version 5.0.

Lowe, Kelly Fisher (2006) *The Words and Music of Frank Zappa*. Westport, Connecticut: Praeger.

Mainieri, Mike (1995) Liner notes, *An American Diary*, NYC 6015-2.

Mainieri, Mike, NYC Records. *http://nycrecords.com*

Marquez, Sal (1994) uncredited interview in 'Frank Zappa', *Musician*, February: 22.

Marsh, Steve (2007) 'Kurt McGettrick – Bari Sax Master R.I.P.', *Sax on the Web*.
http://forum.saxontheweb.net/bulletin/showthread.php?t=59044 *KurtMcgettrick*

Mattingly, Rick (1982) 'Aynsley Dunbar', *Modern Drummer*, May: 8-11, 36, 38, 40, 42-43, 45.

Mattingly, Rick (1982) 'Ed Mann: Expanding Percussion', *Modern Drummer*, August- September: 14-17, 74-77, 79.

Mattingly, Rick (1994) 'Terry Bozzio: Solo Drummer', *Modern Drummer*, July: 21-25, 56-58, 60, 63-64, 66-67.

Mattis, Olivia (2006) 'From Bebop to Poo-Wip: Jazz Influences in Varèse's Poème Elecronique', pp. 309-17 in Felix Meyer and Heidi Zimmerman (eds), *Edgar Varèse: Composer, Sound Sculptor, Visionary*. Woodbridge: Boydell.

McNab, Malcolm (2006) Liner Notes, *Exquisite: The Artistry of Malcolm McNab*, Kinnell House Records KHR 1001.

Menn, Don (1993) 'The Mother of All Interviews', *Guitar Player Presents – Zappa!* : 28-64.

Metalitz, Steve (1974) 'Spotlight on George Duke: An Underexposed Mother', *Downbeat*, 7 November, p. 14.

Milano, Dominic (1978) 'Backstage with Allan Zavod', *Contemporary Keyboard*, April: 8, 48-50.

Milano, Dominic and Doerschuk, Bob (1988) 'Patrick O'Hearn's Mum Thinks He's a Lousy Keyboard Player', *Keyboard*, September: 66-67, 69-72.

Miles, Barry (2004) *Zappa: A Biography*. New York: Grove Press.

Milkowski, Bill (1995) *Jaco: The Extraordinary and Tragic Life of Jaco Pastorius (1st edition)*. San Francisco: Miller Freeman.

Milkowski, Bill (1999) *Rockers, Jazzbos and Visionaries*. New York: Billboard Books.

Moore, Steve (2001) 'Interview with Don Preston', *http://www.stevemoore.addr.com/donpreston.html*

Murray, Charles Shaar (2003) 'Jazz from Hell', *Jazz File*, BBC Radio 3, 22, 29 November, 6 December.

Myers, Marc (2013) 'Shorty Rogers: Rock Sessions', *JazzWax*, 24 June. *http://www.jazzwax.com/2013/06/shorty-rogers-rock-sessions.html*

Nicholson, Stuart (1998) *Jazz-Rock: A History*. Edinburgh: Canongate.

Obermanns, Norbert (1982) *Zappalog (2nd Edition)*. Los Angeles: Rhino Books.

O'Brian, Robert (1984) 'It Just Might be Frank', *RockBill*, November: 14-15, 18-19.

O'Dell, Tom (2009) *Frank Zappa: The Freak-Out List*. Prism

Films/Chrome Dreams Media.

Orloff, Kathy (1970) 'Sound Track', *The Hollywood Reporter*, 21 January.

Otis, Johnny (1993) *Upside Your Head! Rhythm and Blues on Central Avenue*. Middletown: Wesleyan University Press.

Palermo, Ed (2007) 'Zappa and Jazz', *All About Jazz*, 23 December.
*http://www.allaboutjazz.com/php/article.php?id=27819*Zappa and Jazz*

Parker, Scott (2007) *Hungry Freaks Daddy: The Recordings of Frank Zappa and the Mothers Of Invention Volume One 1959-1969*. Waterbury, Connecticut: Scott Parker Books.

Reisner, Robert (1962) *Bird: The Legend of Charlie Parker*. New York: Bonanza, Citadel.

Rense, Rip (1996) Liner notes, *Frank Zappa: The Lost Episodes*, Rykodisc RCD 40573.

Resnicoff, Matt (1991) 'Poetic Justice: Frank Zappa Puts Us in our Place', *Musician*, November: 66-68, 70, 72-77.

Ripe, Cherry (1976) 'At Last the Truth can be Told: Frank Zappa has no Underwear', *New Musical Express*, 17 April, p. 11.

Rounce, Tony (2004) Liner notes, *Jesse Belvin: Guess Who: The RCA Victor Recordings,* Ace CDCH2 1020.

Ruby, Jay (1970) 'Frank Zappa Interview', *Jazz and Pop*, August: 20-24.

Rule, Greg (1991) 'Survivors of the Black Page', *Drums and Drumming*, March: 55-59.

Russell, George (2001) [1953] *The Lydian Chromatic Concept of Tonal Organization*. Fourth edition (second printing, corrected, 2008). Brookline, Massachusetts: Concept Publishing.

Russo, Greg (2003) *Cosmik Debris: The Collected History and Improvisations of Frank Zappa: The Son of Revised*. Floral Park, NY: Crossfire Publications.

Russo, Greg (2012) Liner notes, *Paul Buff: Highlights from the Pal and Original Sound Studio Archives*, Crossfire 9516-2.

Schifrin, Lalo (2004) uncredited interview in 'All Back to My Place', *Mojo*, July: 9.

Schuller, Gunther (1995) Liner notes, *Stan Kenton: City of Glass*, CD reissue, Capitol Jazz 72438 32084 2 5.

Siders, Harvey (1972) 'Meet the Grand Wazoo', *Downbeat*, 9 November, pp. 13, 36.

Simms, Den, Buxton, Eric and Samler, Rob (1990) 'They're doing the Interview of the Century – Part 1', *Society Pages*, 1, April: 14-37.

Simms, Den, Buxton, Eric and Samler, Rob (1990) 'They're doing the Interview of the Century – Part 2, *Society Pages,* 2, June: 16-38.

Simosko, Vladimir and Tepperman, Barry (1974) *Eric Dolphy: A Musical Biography and Discography.* Washington: Smithsonian Institution Press.

Skene, Gordon (2010) 'Weekend Gallimaufry – Frank Zappa's Mount St. Mary's Concert – 1963', *Crooks and Liars*, 14 November. *http://crooksandliars.com/gordonskene/weekend-gallimaufry-frank-zappa*

Skene, Gordon (2011) 'Weekend Gallimaufry – Frank Zappa and Zubin Mehta Talk Music', *Crooks and Liars*, 19 November. *http://crooksandliars.com/gordonskene/weekend-gallimaufry-frank-zappa*

Slaven, Neil (1996) *Electric Don Quixote: The Definitive Story of Frank Zappa.* London: Omnibus Press.

Sloots, Kaspar (2012) *Frank Zappa's Musical Language.* *http://www.zappa-analysis.com/4thedition.htm*

Sparke, Michael (2010) *Stan Kenton: This is an Orchestra!* Denton, Texas: University of North Texas Press.

Spellman, A.B. (1967) *Four Lives in the Bebop Business.* London: MacGibbon & Kee.

Teachout, Terry (2013) *Duke: The Life of Duke Ellington.* London: Robson Press.

Tolleson, Robin (1981) 'Terry Bozzio: Burnin'', *Modern Drummer*, November: 22-24, 94-97.

Ulrich, Charles and Naurin, Jon (2002) 'An Interview with Petit Wazoo Trumpeter Gary Barone', *The Planet of my Dreams*. *http://members.shaw.ca/fz-pomd/wazoo/barone.html*

Underwood, Lee (1977) 'Ian Underwood: Freelance Energizer', *Downbeat*, 19 May, pp. 18-20

Underwood, Lee (1978) 'Profile: L. Shankar', *Downbeat*, 2 November, pp. 42-44.

Underwood, Ruth, Bozzio, Terry, Humphrey, Ralph, Thompson, Chester and Wackerman, Chad (2009) *The Drummers of Frank Zappa*. Oxnard, CA: Drum Channel.

Volgsten, Ulrik (1999) *Music, Mind and the Serious Zappa: The Passions of a Serious Listener*. Stockholm University: Studies in Musicology 9, 1999/2009.

Walley, David (1996) *No Commercial Potential: The Saga of Frank Zappa and the Mothers Of Invention (3rd edition)*. New York: Da Capo.

Watson, Ben (1994) *Frank Zappa: The Negative Dialectics of Poodle Play*. London: Quartet.

Welch, Jane (1970) 'Europe's Answer to Woodstock: The First Actuel Paris Music Festival', *Downbeat*, 22 January, pp. 16-17, 31.

Wictor, Thomas (2001) *In Cold Sweat: Interviews with Really Scary Musicians*. New York: Limelight.

Williams, Richard (2000) *Long Distance Call: Writings on Music*. London: Aurum Press.

Wills, Geoff (2009) 'Don't Gonna Play That Kling-Kling Jazz: A Prehistory of Jazz-Rock', *jazz.com* *www.jazz.com/features-and-interviews/2009/6/18/a-prehistory-of-jazz-rock**

Wills, Geoff (2009) 'Don Preston', *jazz.com* *www.jazz.com/encyclopedia/preston-don-donald-ward*

Wills, Geoffrey I. (2013) 'Zappa and the Story Song: A Rage of Cultural Influences', pp. 117-131 in Paul Carr (ed), *Frank Zappa and the And*. Farnham: Ashgate.

Wolf, Peter (2010) Liner notes, *Frank Zappa: Hammersmith Odeon*, Vaulternative Records VR 20101.

Woodward, Bob (1985) *Wired: The Short Life and Fast Times of John Belushi*. New York: Simon and Schuster.

Zappa, Frank (1963) 'Concerto for Two Bicycles, Pre-Recorded Tape and Instrumental Ensemble', *The Steve Allen Show*, Channel 5 TV, 27 March.
http://www.youtube.com/watch?v=1MewcnFL-6Y

Zappa, Frank (1963) 'Mount St. Mary's Concert', KPFK FM, Los Angeles, 19 May. *www.youtube.com/watch?v=IPJrzpmH2XK*

Zappa, Frank (1967) 'My Favorite Records', *Hit Parader*, August: 61.

Zappa, Frank (1972) *Warner Bros. Circular # 40*, 9 October, pp.2-6.

Zappa, Frank (1972) 'Little Dots', recorded Harper College, Binghampton, 29 October.
www.youtube.com/watch?v=36Umv3bXi5M

Zappa, Frank with Occhiogrosso, Peter (1989) *The Real Frank Zappa Book*. London; Picador.

DISCOGRAPHY

Adderley, Cannonball (1960) *Them Dirty Blues* Riverside RLP 12-322.

Adderley, Cannonball (1960) *Cannonball Adderley at The Lighthouse*. Riverside RLP 9344.

Adderley, Cannonball (1961) *African Waltz*. Riverside RLP 377.

Adderley, Cannonball (1971) *The Black Messiah*. Capitol SWBO-846.

Amy, Curtis (1962) *Tippin' on Through*. Pacific Jazz ST-62.

Anthony, Ray (1958) 'Peter Gunn'. Capitol CL 14929.

Ayler, Albert (1964) *Vibrations*. Debut DEB144.

Ayler, Albert (1968) *New Grass*. Impulse AS9175.

Barron, Louis and Bebe (1976) *Forbidden Planet (Soundtrack)*. Planet Records PR-001.

Barry, John (1960) 'Beat for Beatniks'. Columbia DB 4446.

Baxter, Les (1997) *Black Sunday (Soundtrack)*. Citadel STC 77110.

Beck, Jeff (1977) *Jeff Beck with the Jan Hammer Group – Live*. Epic PE 34433.

Beiderbecke, Bix (2001) *Riverboat Shuffle*. Naxos Jazz Legends 8.120584.

Blake, Ran (2005) *Indian Winter*. Black Saint 121327-2.

Blood, Sweat and Tears (1968) *Child is Father to the Man*. Columbia CS 9619.

Blood, Sweat and Tears (1968) *Blood, Sweat and Tears*. Columbia CK 9720.

Bohuslan Big Band (2000) *Bohuslan Big Band plays Zappa*. Imogena 089.

Bollani, Stefano (2004) *Smat Smat*. Label Bleu LBLC 6665.

Bollani, Stefano (2014) *Sheik yer Zappa*. Decca 0602547051523.

Bozzio, Terry (2005) *Chamber Works*. PAR Media Music ZZ-05GP000 1901.

Brecker Brothers, The (1978) *Heavy Metal Bebop*. Arista AB-4185.

Brown, Boots (1958) 'Cerveza'. RCA 20-7269.

Brown, James (1967) *James Brown at the Latin Casino*. King LP 1018.

Brubeck, Dave (1957) *Dave Digs Disney*. Columbia CL 1059.

Buff, Paul (2012) *Highlights from the Pal and Original Sound Studio Archives*. Crossfire 9516-2.

Chaloff, Serge (1990) *The Fable of Mabel*. Black Lion BLCD760923.

Charles, Ray (1960) 'One Mint Julep'. ABC 19503.

Clarke, Stanley (1974) *Stanley Clarke*. Nemperor NE 431.

Clarke, Stanley (1976) *School Days*. Nemperor NE 439.

Cobham, Billy (1973) *Spectrum*. Atlantic SD 7268.

Cobham, Billy and Duke, George (1976) *Live on Tour in Europe 1976*. Atlantic 50316.

Coleman, Ornette (1961) *Free Jazz*. Atlantic SD-1364.

Coleman, Ornette, Cherry, Don, Giuffre, Jimmy and Dorham, Kenny (2009) *The Lenox Jazz School Concert, August 29, 1959*. Free Factory 064.

Coltrane, John (1961) *My Favorite Things*. Atlantic SD-1361.

Coltrane, John (1961) *Africa/Brass*. Impulse AS-6.

Conniff, Ray (1956) *'S Wonderful*. Columbia CL 925.

Corea, Chick (1975) *The Leprechaun*. Polydor PD 6062.

Davis, Eddie Lockjaw (1961) *Trane Whistle*. Prestige PR 7206.

Davis, Miles (1956) *Birth of the Cool*. Capitol T-762.

Davis, Miles (1960) *Sketches of Spain*. Columbia CL 1480.

Davis, Miles (1970) *Bitches Brew*. Columbia GP 26.

Davis, Miles (2003) *In Person Friday and Saturday Nights Complete*. Columbia Legacy C4K 87106.

Dolphy, Eric (1964) *Out to Lunch*. Blue Note BLP 4163.

Duke, George (1970) *Save the Country*. Pacific Jazz LA 819H.

Duke, George (1971) *The Inner Source*. MPS(G) 68123.

Duke, George (1975) *I Love the Blues, She Heard my Cry*. MPS MC25671.